Sylvia

Book Two

(Children of the Myth Machine)

Enslaving others is for the weak...

Prologue

The Cinn group, one of the most powerful
business organisations in the galaxy, wants control of
all the Children of the Myth Machines for their company
Delve Mining. Only the draoi ársa stand in their way.
The draoi ársa are intent on destroying all the machines
the geneticist Larry Smide built and ending the
merciless cloning for the purpose of slavery.

For the Children of the Forest, the machines are
their beginning. And this is their story...

Chapter One

"*One-seven-ten generations to make us what we are,*" Sylvia sings in the darkness of the forest as she collects strawberries into a wicker basket. She looks up past the branches of a redwood cedar tree to the early summer sky. "*Stories of our ancestors no bigger than an adult hand,*" she continues looking down the laces of her yellow cotton shirt, past the hemp belt that holds up her matching linen skirt to the soft brown fur that covers her human shaped feet. "*Then we grew and grew until our great-grandfather stood as tall as a badger.*" A flying red squirrel glides from one of the redwood's lower branches to an adult maple. Nearby she can hear the sound of bumblebees and the hurried thrum sound of a hummingbird.

"*Two-six-nine are we fully grown yet?*" Her lilting voice travels through the trees as she heads back to the hamlet. "*Grandfather was as tall as my knee, and father stood up to my waist. How tall will my children be?*" she sings as a strong wind pushes against her back. Darkness follows, casting the early morning glimmer into shadow.

She turns around and blinks as loose dirt, leaves and her own long golden brown hair whip into her face. She has seen this once before. Two silver coloured lights the shape of a trillium hurtle out of the sky. She spreads her left hand onto the rough bark of a sugar maple tree and sees her pupils reflect off her hand. She remembers the first time she saw her eyes in a stream. The pupils black and shaped like a birch tree without its leaves. The iris green like grass that sways in an endless wind. Her mother once said the tree-shaped pupils of her eyes grow harlequin green when she is excited, just like her sister Miya's would.

She sends warning pheromones into the sugar maple's bark and waits for them to reach its sapwood. The Children of the Forest know where to run. Since her sister was taken she has made sure they are all prepared. Her father and mother had given up since Miya's capture. She doesn't know where they travelled to but the Children of the Forest have named her Abnoba in her mother's absence. She stares down between her breasts where pebbles of onyx and quartz rest, held in place by a silver necklace made long ago by one of the dwarves. Mother of the Forest Children they call it.

Her hand stays on the maple until her lapin ears hear the cloven hooves of Laurent enter the forest followed by the lighter sound of his young son

Galen, and his father Hettle. She watches as Laurent ducks his trim human torso under low branches. His slick ringlets of raven hair fall around his bare chest. Galen arrives next, only ten seasons old and nearly as tall as his father. Lastly, Hettle appears, shortest of all and huffing from the exertion.

"Them?" Laurent asks in rage and fear in his deep voice.

Sylvia nods. She hurts so much inside she can hardly talk. She glances along Laurent's cloven hooves and the reddish brown fur of his legs that reaches to his abdomen. The hooves are much larger than a deer's. Otherwise, Laurent would not be able to walk on only two legs.

"Go to the safe place!" He commands his son.

Galen glances around with wild eyes. "Go!" Laurent says again with urgency.

"Come," Hettle says in a high voice.

Sylvia removes her hand from the bark. "Find Daryl and get his family to hook up the nets," she tells Laurent.

"If I can wake them up," she hears Laurent reply with a grumble. Eight dwarves march towards her with granite hammers attached to oak shafts and held together with sisal.

"Lana told us you called. Them again?" asks the lead dwarf in his deep, rumbling voice that sounds like he is speaking through his teeth. He runs his thick fingers through his long black beard.

"Yes, Rumbleton," Sylvia replies staring into the distance where the two silver lights shine through the trees where they have landed.

"They must be in collusion with the orcs," Rumbleton grumbles taking a sip from a skin pouch that hangs from his side. Sylvia can smell huckleberry ale on his breath.

"You could try peace," she says reaching down for the skin. Rumbleton and every other dwarf smell of sweat and their bare, bulging chests are covered in rock dust.

"We were made to fight orcs," he replies as he hands her the skin, "and goblins."

A song Sylvia's mother use to sing to her and her sister echoes inside her head and she sings: *The mad creator made us in a machine; made us from*

*living creatures; made us from Nature's own
children.*"

"Don't start on that again," Rumbleton tells
her with a heavy sigh but the others are listening so
she continues.

"*Made to hate; made to please; we are the
Children of Myth,*" she continues.

"There you have it," Rumbleton says with a
grumble. "We were made to hate."

"Try not to," Sylvia tells him, her birch tree
pupils radiating harlequin green so brightly she can
see their image reflecting on Rumbleton's forehead.

"Another day," he says pointing his hammer
in the direction of the two lights, "but first we deal
with them."

"We do it my way!" Sylvia reminds him, her
lilting voice stern.

"Aye," she hears Rumbleton reply with
another grumble, "We hide."

Sylvia smiles at him before turning with a
flourish, her long golden brown hair whipping across
her face. She alone heads in the direction of the
lights from the sky.

She misses her sister so much these days.
They used to play catch within the forest. Miya was
always trying to get her into the prickly bramble
shrubs of blackberries or raspberries so her hair
would get caught. Afterwards Miya would pick out
all the thorny twigs. *"Grind the wheat with a pestle,"*
she sings quietly, *"Add water and roll it into dough"*.
The wind in the forest dies down as she moves from
one tree trunk to the next. *"Add berries or slice the
apples thin."* Her lapin ears make out human voices.
"Roll a top and you have a pie!" She stops singing
and creeps closer to the voices.

"Thrain thinks he knows where the machine
is," she hears the metallic voice that sounds like a
hated human's. She glances around a sugar maple
tree and through a cluster of sumacs. Two humans
in shiny grey suits with white helmets are gazing
around through an auburn visor that makes their
faces impossible to see. Ten paces behind them is a
huge and strange looking metal object with a very
tall cylindrical centre surrounded by four smaller
tubes. From the central cylinder a plank descends
and an opening appears. The ground is scorched all
around the object. Sitting against the trunk of a

beech tree she sees a very tall man in a grey jumper suit with bound hands and feet.

"You heard what he said on the ship," says a short, stalky man as he glances at the tied man while he removes his helmet and gloves. He runs his thick fingers through stubby blond hair.

"I heard," the taller man replies as he too takes off his gloves and helmet. Raven coloured hair falls thickly around his shoulders, 'You want to go where I come from.'

"We know he is or was the King of Terra Cataractarum on that planet Terra Verte," the shorter man says. "When we ask his name he only ever says he is the King or that we may call him Your Highness. Thrain should have cut his tongue out after he cut the jewel out of his belly."

"No matter," the taller one says. "We just need him to show us where the Smide machine is then we can let him go."

A vicious smile crosses the shorter man's face. The taller one whistles and four more men dressed exactly the same way step out of the giant cylinder. They all carry lethal looking metallic cross-bows strapped to their backs. In sheaths on their left side are swords with plain looking hilts.

"*We were created in malice by Smide,*" Sylvia sings under her breath. "*And our ancestors met themselves over and over again.*" She watches as the men remove their grey suits. Underneath they wear green shirts and khaki pants. "*To meet yourself, to fight yourself, over, and over again.*" She squints and notices the shorter of the first two men has a circle within a circle within a circle tattooed on the back of his neck. The taller one, with long raven hair is wearing a gold ring with an onyx stone on his left ring finger.

"Thrain said it has been ten years since Delve Mining last came to Lilly," the shorter man with the circle tattoos says as he scans the area in front of him.

"How old did he say those dreadnaught satellites are?" the taller man asks.

"He said they were put into the atmosphere here a millennium ago by a society of scientists and entrepreneurs called Draoi ársa. And those satellites replenish. They have mechanical scavengers that attach to meteorites on the Harvest Meteorite Belt to extract minerals to repair and rebuild."

"So no gunfire, no laser, and no communication devices outside of the pod?" the taller man asks.

"If we do, the satellites will blast the user to smithereens. We don't want to capture any of these abominations; we just want the Smide machine." The shorter one waves at the other men and they spread out.

Sylvia moves farther back. She can't see them as well but she can still hear them.

"If Delve Mining captures the original cloning machine we lose our livelihood," the tall one says.

"Once we get the Smide machine," the short one tells him, "we get a very nice commission and a guarantee of yearly payments for twenty years."

"Not until death?" the taller one asks.

The smaller one laughs. "And have an accident? No, by that time our investments will make us nicely rich for life. Personally, I would like to hunt these Children of Myth down. Rid the Milky Way of unnatural monsters."

"But the Smide machine will still be in use." The tall one says.

"They're no taller than your hand, maybe some as tall as your knee, when they come out. And they either kill each other in the arenas or die working the mines. I hear they'll all be sterilized this time. Maybe a few will be allowed to have children for those sick individuals that want them as sex slaves." He spits on the ground.

"Kinda sad to hear about all those lives lost," the tall one says with a hint of melancholy in his voice.

"Humans are the only species with a soul."

"They're half human," argues the tall one.

"Still, they don't have a soul," the shorter one says with no doubt in his voice.

"I have no soul," Sylvia says to herself with a chuckle. She puts her hand on the beech tree's trunk. Pheromones flow from her through the bark into its roots and leaves so every plant it connects to can pass on the message—*set the traps!*

"I see a green light coming from those sumacs," the shorter human says.

Sylvia turns around and dashes back into the woods.

"I saw something moving," she hears one of the men say. She can hear the pounding of their feet as she dashes from one tree to another. She runs around an oak tree to where a cluster of buckthorn bushes grow. "Ouch," she shouts out as she drops to one knee to make it sound as if she tripped. The human with the onyx ring and two others run towards her.

She hears them curse as they become entangled amongst the thorns hidden by the little red berries of the buckthorn. It's the third human she focuses on now. She hears a drawstring tightening. She jumps to her left as a cross-bow bolt thuds a pace from her feet. The two humans in the buckthorn are moving freely now. She dashes through sumac and around a dogwood shrub where she places her hand on an oak tree and stares at the bark. *Don't let them see my eyes, don't let them see my eyes.* The pheromones pour out of her and she feels drained.

She notices that the tall man with the onyx ring has seen her; he lets loose a bolt. The bolt sticks into the bark. There is something in his violet eyes that causes her to hesitate before she darts off again.

She needs the humans to chase her to Whispering Stream. The long strands of a weeping willow's leaves are just visible through the forest growth. Her nose twitches at the smell of skunkweed. She hesitates. Her heart pounds so hard she wonders if the humans can hear it. This is life or death now but she forces herself to wait. Her left ear twitches. Two humans are coming at her from the left and the one with the onyx ring, almost inaudible, from the right.

Bolts thud a number of paces from her. She doesn't know if they are trying to herd her or just hoping for a lucky shot. She slips into a grouping of bulrushes and watercress. Both her ears twitch as she looks at her right hand to see if there is any light emitting from her pupils. A fading green image of two birch trees appears on her palm. She hears a rustling sound. One of Mocasín de agua's children slithers across the water.

"Snake!" she hears one of the humans whisper along with the sound of a knife being slid out of its sheath. She wants to shoo the young snake away but can't so she dashes out of the bulrushes towards the nearest weeping willow.

She hears splashing behind her. *Please let Laurent and the dwarves be ready, please!*

"Circle her!" one of the men shouts. She feels a hand grab a hold of her left ankle. Terrified she yanks it free and runs to an opening surrounded by catalpa and beech trees. The three humans are following so close she can hear their heavy breaths and pounding feet. There is a deep twang sound before heavy netting falls on her and the humans. Between the strands she sees Laurent step forward with an ash staff sharpened at one end. She can just make out a few of the dwarves with their stone headed hammers.

Laurent lifts the edge of the net closest to her and she scrambles out. One human is let out at a time so their wrists can be bound with sisal twine. The human with the onyx ring and violet eyes does not struggle but the other two do. She sees glee in Rumbleton's eyes as he strikes their arms and legs with his hammer.

Sylvia peers up into the trees. She squints and sees a three fingered paw with tremendously long fingernails encircle branches from high above. "Thank you Daryl and also your family," she calls up.

"Welcome," a male's voice with a lisp replies. Daryl's face appears through the foliage; his deep set eyes, black dog nose and nearly chinless face smile down at her.

"The pointy-eared one, Lent and his group, have gone after the other humans," Rumbleton tells her with a grin as the humans are blindfolded with black cotton strips normally used by the dwarves to tie their hair back when they forge. Their mouths are gagged with belts made of catfish skin.

"He'll leave us if you keep at him like that," Sylvia warns.

"Good, Lent and his people are too high and mighty for my liking," Rumbleton replies. "I like the make of these cross-bows and knives," he says hefting one in his hand. "Not much use for the swords but you could use them." She hears the underlining protective croak in Rumbleton's voice and smiles back at him.

She is used to the musty smell of the dwarves but the human smell reeks of fear, except for the tall raven haired one with the onyx ring. His scent has little acidity to it. "*Walking in the Spring"* she sings as the dwarves force the humans to walk. "*Along the river bank. Near the budding branches of the magnolia."* She glances back at the man with the onyx ring as she continues to sing. His head is tilted in her direction. "*The smell of wet soil,"* she continues. "*Time of new life."*

She sings until they come to a glade surrounded by sandstone boulders covered in pincushion moss. She sees Lent and three other elves waiting for them with the man with the three rings tattooed on his neck, the other two slavers, and the mysterious, very tall man, with the sickly blue skin that looks as if it should be black. All four men are gagged and their feet and hands tied.

She sees welts across the face of the man with the three ring tattoo. "He is their leader," she says pointing at him.

"Interesting, he's the daftest of them," Lent tells her. His lynx ears twitch in annoyance. His upturned black eyebrows make him look snooty but she has always been attracted to the epicanthic skinfold that give his eyes a slanted look. "But the very tall one with the sickly blue hue to his skin

seems more like the leader." Lent undoes the belt
from the mouth of the man with the tattoos.

"Get away from me you freakish
abomination!" the man shouts as spittle flies from his
mouth. "You will die! Die and then I'll have you re-
made and killed again!"

"Not likely," Lent replies smugly, "that was
our ancestors from many years ago. We are born."

The face of the man reddens as he strains his
head forward. "I will find every one of you pointy
eared creeps and have lead poured into your impotent
mouths." He peers around wildly until he catches
sight of Laurent. "All your children will be murdered
before your eyes. I will--." Sylvia is very frightened
by the man but no one threatens the Children of the
Forest. She puts all her weight behind a heel kick to
the man's forehead. The back of his head smashes
into the rock he is tied against. She has never killed
before. The idea that she might now have stuns her.
She doesn't know if she feels it is wrong or is
indifferent. The man's head lists to the right. She
sees blood on the stone where the back of his head
made contact. She hears him swear under his
breath. He lifts his head and smiles at her. "Wait

until the group from the other pod find out we're not sending a return signal." His eyes roll back to white and his chin flops onto his chest.

Lent walks over to the very tall man and undoes the belt around his mouth. "You seem wiser," Lent says to him with a surprising amount of courteousness.

"There will be more," the very tall man says in a tired but powerful and deep voice as he glances into the sky.

Sylvia smells something burning. She turns around to see that all the other men but the one with the onyx ring are pointing a silver button sewn on their right sleeve at her. She sees the sisal bindings around their wrists fall to the ground with burnt ends. A tiny red light points at her chest. "Shouldn't mess with technologically superior races," one of the humans tells her smugly. She goes to dart away when there is a yellow flash from the sky. She drops to the ground and covers her head.

The smell of burnt flesh makes her feel sick. She opens her eyes and looks at the incinerated corpses of four of the humans. Only the very tall man, the short man with the circle tattoos, and the onyx ring man are still alive. She glances around at the other Children of the Forest. There is shock in their eyes but they are otherwise fine.

"When will the others arrive?" she asks the very tall man.

"Call him Your Highness when you address him and if he wants to talk to you he'll speak first," the man with the onyx ring tells her.

Sylvia fixes her gaze on the man with the sickly bluish skin. "He is normally right," the very tall man replies in a rumbling, raspy voice.

"Why are you here?" she asks, glancing at the unconscious man with the three circles.

"They brought me here to find a cruel machine," he replies staring directly at her. The irises of his eyes are a mix of colours, blue around the border and brownish-green in the centre. She forces herself not to become lost in the endlessness of his stare.

"What machine?" she manages to ask.

"The machine that created your ancestors," he replies.

Sylvia steps back in surprise. "That machine is our beginning!"

"Yes, but you have evolved since then," he says with a wan smile that makes him look skeletal. "You were born, not created from a machine."

Sylvia recalls the time she saw Jezzel, Laurent's wife, with Galen as a baby at her breast. She had felt so jealous as Jezzel cooed at her baby and sang soft melodies to him. Sylvia also knew that Galen was a miracle baby. Jezzel, as an equine satyress, did not know if she could mate with Laurent. Their first three children came out badly deformed, with bodies of both horse and deer and human in a combination that did not survive. Jezzel told Sylvia she feared her togetherness with Laurent would be barren of children. It was common among Children of the Forest to have miscarriages or deformed babies that did not live long. Sylvia wondered who she could mate without having to see her babies die from the mix of rabbit, tree, and human within her. The dwarves, elves and other original creations of the machine didn't have nearly as many miscarriages when they kept to their own. But she and her sister were like no others she knew of. "Where did the others land?"

The very tall man turns his head and stares at the man with onyx ring. Sylvia also turns her attention to him. "By the setting of your sun, north of here," the man says.

"Orc and goblin territory," Rumbleton says with a laugh.

"The dreadnaught satellites will not let us use scanners here so we separated," the man with onyx ring says. "One group with the King," he looks at the very tall man, "and one group hoping to capture and...talk to sentient beings to find the machine."

"Why do you want the machine?" Laurent asks.

The man with the onyx ring stares at the ground as he says in a voice full of remorse, "To have an endless amount of slaves."

"Our ancestors were no taller than a hand, with only a few twice that," Laurent tells him.

"Yes, I've heard, and easy to replace," the man with the onyx ring adds. "Cloning full sized individuals takes a lot more material and time."

"Why are there not more of these machines?" Laurent asks and Sylvia can hear the despair in his voice.

"No one has been able to duplicate them. I looked up the creator of the Children of Myth machines, Larry Smide, before we came here. May I have some water?" the man with the onyx ring asks as he stares longingly at a water skin tied around Laurent's left shoulder. Sylvia sees Laurent hesitate as Rumbleton scowls. Laurent glances at her. She nods and he pours some water into the man's mouth then he gives the very tall man the rest.

"Continue," Sylvia insists.

"He was a selfish biochemist and genetic engineer who loved to mix human, animal, and plant genetics together. He was banned by the rest of society and sent to prison. Delve Mining saw potential in his work so ensured that he was relocated to a new penal colony; one they controlled. They moved him to a small penal world where he could do as he pleased. And it pleased him to try and create more fictional characters. Smide had one friend on the planet with him, Carl Peters, an energy engineer who destroyed an entire factory building with one of his illegal experiments. On the planet Peters was working on a project to make items last indefinitely. He learned to harness nuclear energy with super conduction into items like rings, swords, flashlights made of stone, and other devices. Smide tricked Peters into building him an energy source for a project he was working on, never telling him that it was for the Children of Myth machine.

"When Peters found out he tried to destroy the machine but it was impossible. The machine has an endless amount of energy and protects itself with a force field. Frustrated Peters set out to build a device to engulf the Children of Myth machine, so Smide could no longer use it. Something went wrong while he built the new machine because an explosion that started in his shop destroyed the crust of the planet. The only things that remained unscathed in the debris of the exploded planet were the Children of Myth machine and numerous of his devices, two of them living. Generations later those devices still work. They're worth more than I can imagine and are known as Relics or Artefacts."

"That means," the man with the circle tattoos adds with a parched voice full of venom, "you have no souls. Just like the human clones."

"You didn't kick him hard enough, Sylvia," Rumbleton tells her, raising his hammer.

"Why don't you give us your names?" Sylvia asks with one hand up to Rumbleton.

"Ask His Highness, he's never given us a name," says the man with the circle tattoos.

"I will call him Daft," Rumbleton says pointing his hammer at the man with the circle tattoos. "And him Raven," he points at the man with the onyx ring, "And him," he begins but hesitates not quite lifting his hammer high enough to point at the King. "Him we'll call Rex."

"Laurent, will you gag Daft?" Sylvia asks. She hears the dwarves chuckling. "Who will guard them?" she asks.

"You're going to the orc and goblin's foul land?" Rumbleton asks.

"Yes—," she is about to say more when he interrupts her.

"But I'm not. Because I hate them and they certainly hate me. We dwarves will guard." He glances around at the four circles made up of black ash, "What's left of them."

"We can follow but it would be unwise for us to negotiate, if that is your plan," Lent says. "After dwarves they hate elves the most."

"I will go with you," Rex tells her in a tone she knows she cannot refuse.

"And me," Raven adds. "You could use me as a prisoner if necessary."

"Traitor," Daft snarls as he tries to twist his body free of the bindings and from Laurent gagging him.

"We just need the machine," Raven says evenly. "Take care of my friend," he tells Rumbleton.

"Laurent?" Sylvia asks staring into his serious eyes.

"Pogues will go with us and I'll ask Lana," he says with a forlorn look.

She watches him dash off before she turns to the very tall man. "You are a prisoner?"

"He is," Raven answers for him.

"Than he is not our enemy," Sylvia says nodding towards Rumbleton. She looks over at Daft and sees the hate in his eyes. *But you are.* The man gives her mixed emotions. Part of her wants to kick him again, harder, another part just wants to get as far away as possible from him. She sees Rumbleton untie the bindings on Rex with great courteousness.

"What of the metal thing?" Rumbleton asks. "We could strip it for weapons and tools."

"A giant spaceship will be returning in a month, perhaps only a week," Raven says. "There will be more pods landing if you don't give up the Children of the Myth machine."

"We will war!" Rumbleton shouts with such ferociousness that Sylvia cringes.

"Delve Mining will find a way to destroy the Dreadnaught satellites that protect your world," Raven tells Rumbleton with such frankness it disturbs Sylvia. She can tell from the shocked faces on all the other Children of the Forest that Raven's words have the same effect on them. "If that happens there won't be anything to incinerate the next wave of mercenaries when they use their technological weapons."

She catches a measured look in Rex's transfixing stare. To escape his ensorcelling eyes she has to close her own and re-open them elsewhere. "It has an opening," she says to Lent.

"It is still open," Lent tells her. "Very strange inside."

Rex stands up, his height dwarfing all around him. Sylvia does not shudder as she thinks she should; instead she is drawn to him. He is not like the tale of the incubus to the far north but his presence gives her the feeling she had when she was younger listening to the tales of the sabio andantes to the far south.

"The moisture outside could damage the inside of the pod," he says in a voice like muted thunder. Sylvia sees him roll his one foot from side-to-side then the other as he clenches and flexes his hands. *What is the shape of the perfect human* she wonders because he appears to be perfectly proportioned and yet she sees no body hair. His skin colour perplexes her. Is his skin dark blue like the midnight sky, or black as the pupil of an eye?

"Let us pass by it and I will show you how to close the hatch," Raven offers. *And why is this one so compliant* she wonders?

Sylvia hears the sound of hooves getting nearer. She turns around to see Laurent with Pogues hopping beside him. In the air she hears the swishing of wings as Lana lands on the branch of a nearby sugar maple.

"The dwarves, elves, and satyrs all came from the machine," Raven says, his voice sounding confused to Sylvia, "but the rest of you, there is no description in the annals of any of you."

"We're a mix," Pogues tells him with his throaty voice.

"A giant toad with a human torso," Raven says. Sylvia sees him lean closer to Pogues. "Your eyes look human but for the elliptical shape of your pupils, and your nose and mouth are more toad, while your head and hair are human."

"Our mad creator mixed up all different peoples over time," Pogues tells him as he brushes back his thin blond hair.

"But the annals only show that dwarves, elves, orcs, goblins, and satyrs were ever created. Smide died when the planet exploded. He was dead before any of your ancestors could come about." Raven sounds more perplexed. "Nothing says he went beyond the creatures of mythology and fantasy."

"Our creator landed here, with his machine," Pogues replies. "Garth is at least four hundred seasons old and his father lived a thousand seasons, and his grandfather a thousand before him, and so on. The truth is well known to his family. The creator died of madness not on an exploding planet."

Sylvia smiles at the memory of ancient Garth. His carapace has to be three paces by three paces. His extra-long neck just barely holds the weight of his human head. When he wants to talk for a lengthy time he rests his bearded chin on a rock or log.

"Didn't you want revenge?" Raven asks.

"We wouldn't be, if not for him," Pogues replies with a shrug as his long pink tongue whips out and wraps its end around an armoured sow bug. Raven's jaw drops.

"Get some of the stored dried fish," Rumbleton tells another dwarf. "You'll need some supplies in case you can't catch anything on the way," he tells Sylvia.

"Lana can spy for us," Sylvia says with as much assurance in her voice as she can muster. She has no idea how the orcs and goblins will react to them.

"Does the machine still work?" Sylvia asks hoping Pogues will answer based on what Laurent would have told him about the humans on route here.

"No," he lies, "and it sits far to the north where the incubus and succubus thrive," he answers truthfully.

"Humans that drink the blood of their victims after they have sex with them live there?" Raven asks.

"Not completely human," Pogues answers.

"He designed them to be sanguinarians?" Raven sounds disgusted and surprised.

"And gorgeous," says the throaty, sexually charged voice of Lana from the maple tree. "Like him," she says and Sylvia knows she means Rex.

"He's not a vampire," Raven says with a shrug.

But he is perfect, Sylvia thinks.

The dwarf that Rumbleton sent to gather supplies returns with a large flaxen coloured sack that bulges at the bottom. The mouth of the sack is

tied around a short fighting staff for carrying.
"There's enough dried meat for eight
days,"Rumbleton tells her. "There are two water
skins in case yours gets punctured and small bags
with wrapped dates, raisins and last year's walnuts.
I threw in two fleece blankets sewn to canvas to keep
the cold and damp out. I would let Raven carry the
sack," Rumbleton suggests.

"I will," Raven agrees.

Sylvia stares up into the sky. She is
exhausted. "We'll go at first light." She thinks about
the incubus and succubus. "Open your mouth," she
says looking up at Rex. He shows her perfectly
shaped and spaced teeth with no extended canines.
He is so hard to read. She wants to be near him, to
do things for him, but is he simply enchanting her?

Chapter Two

All the humans are tied up for the night. Two dwarves stay awake to stop any attempts to escape and Sylvia knows some of the elves will also be watching between the trees. She rolls into a ball amongst some ferns. Her sleep is tortured in dreams of a dark handsome man wooing her until she lies exposed welcoming him into her arms. She can feel his long fingers trace along her body as he kisses down her throat. She awakes just as his teeth sink into her neck.

Covered in sweat and early morning dew she forces herself up and checks to see if the prisoners are still tied against the boulder. Rex's eyes are open and staring into the sky while Raven and Daft are both sleeping. She slips through the woods to the bank of Whispering Stream. Laurent is sitting upon a willow root with drenched hair talking to Jezzel in a hushed voice as she bathes in an eddy. *Good*, Sylvia thinks, they're both not in the water. She slips off her garments and slides into the water. Laurent and Jezzel notice her at the same time.

"Come over here and share the potpourri scents Laurent and Pogues gathered for me." Jezzel says with a beautiful smile.

"I wish I could dive under like you can," Sylvia says trying to keep water out of her lapin ears as she dog paddles to Jezzel. She slips around the rocks that cause the eddy, keeping her breasts just under the water. She isn't worried about Laurent's reaction to her nudity; she can see how he absolutely adores his wife. "What's in the potpourri?" she asks, her lilting voice lifting, as the swirls of water brush against her skin.

"Lavender," Jezzel tells her. Sylvia watches, amused, as Jezzel looks up at Laurent for confirmation.

"Lemon balm, rosemary, and chocolate mint as well." He adds.

"Can you hold off until Laurent joins you in a while?" Jezzel asks her with a naughty grin.

The desire and desperateness Sylvia sees in Jezzel's eyes make Sylvia envious. "Yes," she replies with her own naughty grin as she swims back to shore to where her clothes are.

Her ears twitch and she hears rustling and tender whispers coming from the bulrushes as she puts on her clothes. She caresses the front of her skirt, remembering better days, when her mother showed her how to dye her clothes green with lilacs.

At the glade she sees everyone ready, each holding their staff with a sack of what they will carry thrown over their shoulders and a skin of water tied crisscross against their chests. "Put it down for now," she tells everyone with a mischievous grin, "Laurent will be...," she pauses for effect, "here shortly."

"Now?!" Rumbleton shouts out with mock anger and the rest of the nearby Children of the Forest laugh. "Maybe he won't be able to journey with you after she's done with him." There is more laughter. Rumbleton grabs a piece of salted catfish and brings it to Rex. "Best to eat a bit before you leave," he says with reverence.

Daft shakes his head violently and makes horrible muffled sounds through his gag. Sylvia backpedals as she sees his face turn red and his eyes bulge. She notices that Rex ignores Daft's antics as he bites into the fish ravenously. She glances at Raven. There is a mixture of concern and curiosity on his face.

Laurent shows up soon after with his staff and sack. He looks complacent but not happy. She can see the idea of travelling to the north sits poorly with him.

First they head towards the human pod when Lent and a few of the other elves appear suddenly out of the forest. "I and Sar will go with him," he says nodding towards Rex.

Sylvia puts her left arm up to stop Raven from following. She watches keenly as Rex, Lent, Sar, and Pogues enter the pod. "Why didn't Daft want him to eat the fish?" she asks Raven.

"We haven't fed him since Terra Three, and I don't know if they gave him anything since he was captured on Terra Verte," he replies with truth in his voice. "Water but no food."

"Why?"

"He will grow strong again with sustenance."

"I can hear your heart beating," Sylvia warns him without knowing why.

Raven's lips move but he seems unable to speak.

"Why are you with us now?" she asks listening intently to the sound of his heart and smelling the acidity of his sweat.

"I wanted to travel. I started off as a mineral finder for Delve Mining and I had some background in security so I volunteered to help find Smide's machine. I heard that—the one you call Daft along with a notorious slaver named Thrain—had captured this very tall individual with an ominous presence. I wanted to meet with him but by that time he was already gagged, shackled and emaciated." Sylvia does not hear any rapid increase in Raven's heart rate or smell any increase in his sweat's acidity.

"What do you know about him?" she asks wanting to be closer to Raven. Images of Jezzel and Laurent burn into her thoughts.

"Nothing," Raven replies with an exasperated sigh.

She catches sight of Rex hunching over as he steps out of the space pod followed by Pogues. Sar comes next and lastly Lent. Lent's right eyebrow is raised and he has a perplexed look on his face. He motions her away from the rest of the group.

"The very tall one Rumbleton named Rex brought up a magical hallucination with lines and circles," he whispers in her left ear. "He tapped some of them and they turned different colours. I tried to follow exactly what he did but his back blocked me. A shelf opened and he grabbed something out of it."

"I'll try to find out," Sylvia whispers back. "I have to relieve myself," she announces and walks into some bushes not far from Rex and Raven.

"But how can they have souls if they can just be reproduced?" she hears Raven ask in his smooth tenor voice.

"Do twins, triplets, quintuplets have souls?" Rex asks in return with his soft baritone voice.

"How many souls can there be?" Raven asks.

She hears nothing for a little while. "There are likely more than a trillion people in the galaxy," Rex replies.

"And numerous religions," Raven adds with a frustrated sound to his voice. "What religion is the soul?"

"If you walked into a room full of babies," she hears Rex ask, "Could you tell what religion any of the babies are?"

"It's impossible to know if you don't know their parent's chosen religion," Raven replies.

"Yet they have souls."

"That thought, Your Highness, would be considered blasphemous on most worlds."

She hears Rex make a quiet chuckle. "Do you know your ancestral home?"

"Earth," Raven replies. "I wasn't born there, that would be Quasant."

"Do you feel a desire to visit Earth?"

"No, but I would like to return to Quasant," Raven answers with a sigh.

"Do you still follow many of the customs of Quasant?"

"Yes, mostly," Raven replies. Sylvia wipes her hands on some dew covered leaves. She can just see the two men conversing through the bush.

"Is it the soul that gives you your culture and religion or the land you come from?"

"I will have to think on that," Raven replies.

Sylvia steps out of the bush. "We have to go," she says. Up in a nearby oak tree she hears Lana's wings fluttering.

Raven grabs a hold of his staff and swings the sack full of their supplies behind his back. Sylvia takes in a deep breath and goes over to Rex. She stares up at him and says, "Walk with me." She hears him chuckle. "What is amusing you," she asks conversationally as she intentionally speeds up to be far ahead of the others.

"You remind me of someone I hope to see soon," he replies and she catches him staring into the sky as he easily keeps up to her rapid pace.

"I am looking for someone too," she says thinking of Miya.

He looks down at her and she feels lost in his gaze. "We will go together," he assures her.

She has to force herself to look away from his absorbing gaze. "What did you do in the ship?" she asks, not looking up at him.

"A man named Thrain, a slaver, has something of mine I want back. When we have found the machine I now have a way of searching for him," he replies in his baritone voice and she hears a hint of violence in it.

"He is the one who wants the Children of Myth machine?" she asks trying to focus on their surroundings and not Rex's hypnotic voice.

"Machines," he replies to her shock. "There are five. The original one is here on Lilly. The other four Smide sold millennium ago to fund his projects."

"Why do they want this one and why did Raven tell me there was only one?" She hopes if Delve Mining knows about the others they will leave Lilly alone.

"Always question the source of your information," Rex replies.

"How did you get yours?" she asks taking a chance and glancing up at him. When he doesn't answer, she asks, "Am I supposed to call you Your Highness to get an answer?"

"I heard your friends refer to you as Abnoba," he replies. "I do not expect you to call me Your Highness."

"So what is your real name?" she asks.

"Rex," he replies and the tone of his voice tells her he doesn't want to talk anymore.

She lets the rest of the party catch up as she leads them north by following the sound of the river Gold. She can't see the river but she remembers its golden hue as the sun casts its rays upon it. *"Follow the river,"* she sings, *"with a thump-thump-thump of the feet; But don't fall in; Don't let the water nymphs pull you down-down-down."* She keeps singing until the twilight makes the surroundings look less green and brown, and more blue as they near the bank of Gold.

Sylvia sees Pogues hop over to the bank and collect rocks. Laurent goes over and helps him carry them to a clearing between a group of willow and beech trees. Sylvia takes a flint knife from the sack Raven is carrying and cuts a circle of sod out. She places the gathered rocks around it. Pogues gives her moss and twigs from the ground while Laurent gathers dead branches off the trees. She scrapes two pieces of flint together until sparks light the dry moss.

"Can I help?" Raven asks.

"Get the dried fish out. We'll skewer them on sticks so we can enjoy them hot. Maybe tomorrow we will catch fresh ones."

She watches him get long sticks with one pointed end from Laurent and spike a fish for each of them. She hears a very soft footstep go into the forest and turns around to see Rex bending over and gathering something in the woods. He returns with blueberries wrapped in a catalpa leaf.

Little is said as the fish cook. Sylvia has Raven hold two sticks of fish over the fire while she and Laurent hold two more. She sees Pogues searching for beetles and other night bugs to eat. When the fish are ready Sylvia brings one of hers to a low hanging branch and gives it to Lana who is perched on a raised oak root. The darkness doesn't do justice to the beautiful red hair of her cousin or the quizzical green eyes with their vertical pupils.

"Daryl and some of his children are making more nets of vines in case we are followed back," Lana tells her in her luscious, throaty voice.

"Anything to worry about?" Sylvia asks, keeping her voice low.

"No, but I will fly ahead tomorrow."

"Thank you," Sylvia says as she goes on her tippy-toes and kisses her cousin's right cheek.

The fire's embers are dying as she returns to the camp. The night grows colder. She takes out a cotton blanket and covers her shoulders with it. She sees Raven shiver and lifts half the cover for him to sit beside her.

Sometime in the night she wakes to find his arms around her, his left under her head and his right splayed on her shirt just below her breasts. He must have awoken for she feels his hand slide under her shirt and onto her left breast. She feels something moving down below on him. His lips brush against her neck. In a flurry she stands up grabbing the blanket with her left hand and his right hand with the other. She leads him deeper into the woods.

She raises her arms as he slides her shirt off. She feels his mouth against hers and meets his tongue as it pushes between her lips. His thumbs rub her nipples as she hastily undoes the buttons of his shirt. One of his hands reaches between her legs and Sylvia forgets that anything else in the world exists.

The first reddish glow of dawn draws her eyes open and she notices something near the bank. Raven is snoring softly beside her. She pulls her garments on and creeps closer to peer through the willows that grow along Gold's shore. A very tall silhouette stands naked. His skin shines more black than blue now as the river's water drips off his perfect body. He is looking up into the sky; his body tense with reserved desperation for whomever he is searching for. She sees two identical purple scars between his shoulder blades. She moves farther back as he turns. He seems completely unconcerned with his nudity. Something on his stomach catches her attention. Where his belly button should have been she sees only a jagged, circular scar. She watches as he puts on his clothes and walks towards the camp.

When she returns Raven gazes at her with craving and something else in his eyes she likes but can't put into words. "Come," she tells him with her right hand reaching out.

She leads him to the river where they both climb into the cool water. She keeps her breasts just below the waterline while he stands tall the water reaching just above his hips. His entire abdomen is covered in a dark grey tattoo of a circle within a circle. Between the circles are triangles, each with a different image. She moves closer to him and traces the images.

"It represents every major event in my life," he tells her.

"There is no wife or children," she says gazing into his eyes.

"That could be my next tattoo," he says slipping into the water so they are face to face. She feels his hands on her legs as he pulls her towards him. She wraps her legs around his waist. She catches him looking down as her nipples glow green through the water.

As they return to the camp Pogues is replacing the sod where the fire has been while Laurent carries the stones back to the bank. She sees a look of betrayal on their faces. "Get the sack!" she commands Raven more sharply than she means to. He must have seen their faces as well because she hears no rebuke from him.

She intends to walk with Rex again but before she does she whispers to Raven, "Give them time to trust."

"I will," he whispers back with a grin. His face becomes shallow. "Check on Mo—Daft, he is craftier than you know."

"It's too late for any of us to go back now." Her heart thuds, Raven's warning will stay with her now.

"What does a circle within a circle within a circle mean?" she asks Rex as they walk ahead.

"Its original name is adinkrahene," he tells her and the power of his baritone voice makes her want to be closer to him. "One of its meanings is great, charismatic leader."

"Is that what Daft is?" she asks keeping her eyes forward. Soon they will be in goblin territory.

"Anyone can get a tattoo, Abnoba," his voice replies with a rumble. "Someday I will introduce you to one who deserves that tattoo."

"Will he escape?" she asks as she glances up into his deep eyes.

"His rage hinders his capabilities but he is devious. He will talk whenever he can, repeating the same thing over and over again so people start to wonder if it is the truth. You may find him free and your people divided when you return."

Sylvia squeezes her eyes closed. Rumbleton and Lent are both known for their strong personalities. She has to have faith in them. The trees are less dense ahead and the jutting granite rocks continue to get larger until it becomes Mons Montis itself. She stops and waits for Pogues to catch up. "This is as far as I have ever been," she says glancing wearily from rock to rock.

"The goblins live in crevices and small caves throughout the rocks." Pogues tells her in his slurping voice. He looks up into the sky. "We need to get over Mons Montis before the sun goes down. The creator gave them eyes to see well into the night."

Raven comes up to her sheathed in sweat from carrying the sack of supplies. "What do they look like?"

he asks breathing heavily and putting the sack down without permission. She sees Raven look up at Rex. Raven's expression turns from tired to shame. When she looks up at Rex she notices an intense look of admonishment on his flawless face.

Rex smiles at her, "This is your kingdom," he tells her and falls silent.

Chapter Three

"They have oversized heads," Pogues tells everyone. "Bat ears, the body of a creature called a panda bear, and legs of a human."

Sylvia notices a confused look cross Raven's face. "That's not what the galactic server shows them to look like, are you sure they are called goblins?" he asks.

Pogues rolls his warty shoulders back. "That's what the creator called them."

Sylvia's ears twitch at the sound of unfamiliar movement from the rocks ahead. A war scream from a dozen voices pounds her eardrums as naked goblins appear on the rocks. They hold javelins, slingshots, or clubs made from the thighbones of large creatures.

Pogues screams back at them. Sylvia and Laurent join him. She hears the swish of wings as Lana prepares to fly from a nearby tree.

"Give me a cross-bow," Raven whispers to her.

"No," she replies keeping her eyes on the goblins. She continues to scream out in anger along with Pogues and Laurent. The goblins stop shouting and glare at them. She can't think of a single description that will summarize all of them. Some have small black, beady eyes and the flat snout of a bat on their oversized heads. Others have large brown eyes surrounded by black fur.

The only similarities are the varying size of their bat wings and large bellies that are covered in black and white fur.

A figure with more grey fur then white, steps forward. "Dwarves and elves are our enemies!" he screams out, his voice sounding canine.

"None of those are here!" Sylvia shouts back.

"We kill and eat you!" the grey one screams, raising his club into the air with a stubby arm and clawed hand.

"You will die if you hinder our passage!" Sylvia warns him. She steps forward.

"You have humans," the grey one says accusingly and spits on the ground.

"Servants," Sylvia replies. She can smell the stench of skin infections from the goblins. Pogues makes a menacing throaty sound as he follows her closer to the goblins.

"That one," the grey goblin says, looking at Rex, but says no more but makes way for Rex as he walks beside Sylvia.

Sylvia keeps a scowl on her face as she glances up at Rex. He is smiling and his deep eyes sparkle with the amusement of a magus as he nods towards the goblins.

Pogues hops up to her. "The orcs will not be so easy to intimidate," he whispers into her ear, "and these are the Mons Montis goblins, mostly herders. On the other side is the Vale de Coníferas goblins, and they are much larger."

Sylvia takes in a deep breath. She squints up at the jagged rocks where snow-white mountain goats stare back down at her.

She hears the distinct sound of Raven's heavy breathing as he labours up to her. "I have only seen them in pictures," he says with awe in his voice. "They look so powerful and majestic with their white beards and curved horns."

Tingles of excitement run through Sylvia's body as he speaks. She wants to tell him he doesn't need to carry the supplies but who else can? Pogues and Laurent already have their own light sacks and staffs along with their weapons to carry. And she needs to be ready for anything. "I have never seen them before," she tells him with true wonderment.

"The Draoi ársa must have brought them here," Raven tells her.

She can see he is struggling to keep up as Rex continues to climb at a constant pace.

"Brought them here?" Sylvia asks. "Is there anything that began here?"

"No," Raven replies. "Everything came from Earth. The Draoi ársa left Earth a millennium ago. You know nothing of this?"

"I know there are aliens, such as yourself," she replies with anger, "who stole my sister and other Children of The Forest."

"I see the wrongs of my way," he admits with tenderness in his voice. "It's why I talk so often to the one you call Rex. He sees the world differently, more clearly than anyone else I have ever met."

"What is your real name?" Sylvia asks as she grabs Raven's right arm and helps him over some rocks.

"Talib, but I am growing fond of Raven. There is a path up ahead."

"Talib," she repeats. She sees the path just as Rex turns towards it. "These Draoi ársa made Lilly?"

"No, the world existed but they made it liveable." She can hear his breathing labour harder as they continue up the stepped path.

Sylvia looks around and notices everyone is tired. The trees here are scarce and stubbier. She sees Lana looking for somewhere to perch. "Stop," she tells everyone. She searches for the tallest tree for Lana to perch on. Rex is already sitting on a flat granite rock. "Can Lana rest on your shoulders?" she asks him.

His engulfing eyes look from her to where Lana tries to find purchase on a white spruce tree without the needles jabbing into her. "Lana," his baritone voice thunders through the air. Sylvia sees her cousin shudder than stare in Rex's direction. He points to his shoulders. Lana glances at the spruce one more time before flapping over to Rex where she gingerly lands on his shoulders.

Lana waves Sylvia over. "It's too bright out here for me during the day," Lana tells her glancing at the disappearing sun.

"Can you get back safely?" Sylvia asks peering at her cousin's orange talons as they dig into Rex's shoulders. It is rare for her to see Lana without the cover of branches and leaves. The long brown feathers of her condor wings cover most of her pale abdomen and breasts when she stands.

"Once twilight is here."

"Tell them Daft is dangerous, not to listen to what he says," she warns.

"I will," Lana replies pushing off from Rex's shoulders as her oversized wings flap. "There is a walnut tree near here where I can land and stay undercover until it is dark enough.”

“Be careful!” Sylvia shouts out to her as her cousin’s wings beat harder to rise higher into the air.

“She is surprisingly light,” she hears Rex say.

“She can’t fly far, even with those long wings of hers,” Sylvia says squinting into the distance at her cousin.

“Her eyes are like yours but not the pupils,” his voice rumbles above her.

“We are cousins.” She says as she hears Pogues hop up behind her.

“I think tomorrow The Mon Montis goblins will bring some of their flock to the Coníferas goblins,” he tells her, glancing at the waning sun. “That’s as much as I have ever gleamed from my travels to here.” She hears the warning in his voice.

“You’ve never found a path into the Coníferas goblins’ land?”

“Never. I don’t think any of the Children of the Forest have been this far. Maybe ancient Garth but I’ve never heard him tell any stories.”

“Hurry,” she says projecting her voice so only the others can hear. With a glance back she sees Raven struggling. Pogues curses and hops over to Raven.

"*There's a time*," she sings in hushes, "*when you have to let determination overrule fear.*" She reaches the peak as twilight covers her. The downward slope of the hill before her and the entire valley below is thick with spruce, cedar and pine. Along the centre of the valley before Mons Montis's smaller brother Mons Brevis are clusters of giant redwoods. *Lana would have liked it here* she thinks before pushing on. "*There's a time, to get on even if you want to scream and hide,*" she sings. She senses something ominous as her hands grasp onto the trunks of spruce trees to slow her descent. The farther down she goes the denser the number of trees become.

She admonishes herself for not telling the others a signal that will bring them together. She could have made up a whistle or animal call. It's too late now.

At the bottom she takes in great gulps of air. Her ears perk up and she hears the laboured breaths of Pogues, Laurent and Raven. Spruce, pine and cedar make up the dominant tree growth here. She doesn't bother trying to use the trees to call the others, only a few of the Children of the Forest can feel her signals and Lana is long gone by now.

Every sound in this forest is unfamiliar to her. She drops into a semi-crouch and moves towards

Pogues' breathing. His human hands are holding onto a pine trunk as he sniffs the air. "Pogues," she calls in little more than a whisper. She catches him smiling at her as she moves behind the tree trunk.

"I can smell Laurent," Pogues tells her in a hushed voice.

"And I Raven but not Rex." She squeezes closer to him. "Let's get Laurent and Raven and hope Rex finds us."

"We may have to leave him," Pogues warns squeezing her hand. "We need to get through the Mons Brevis as quickly as possible."

Sylvia gulps. She pulls her hand away and darts towards Laurent's scent. She finds him with Raven and Rex. As a trial she inhales deeply. This close, Rex's sweat is just discernible.

"We need a signal," she says as Pogues catches up.

"The hoot of an owl," Raven suggests. Rex glares down at him. Raven's eyes lower, "I am sorry. I should wait until you are finished."

"One hoot means wait, two means everything is safe," Sylvia says as her eyes wander to each person.

Pogues sniffs the air. "I can smell them through the fragrance of the pine and cedar."

"You lead," Sylvia says, "next Rex and I."

"What do we do when we reach the Children of Myth machine?" she asks Rex in a hushed voice.

He stares down at her and she feels time stand still. "Take it to Terra Verte."

"What is there?" she asks staring into his eyes as they continue to walk.

A wan smile crosses Rex's face. "My current home and something that will stop the machine from working."

"How do we get it there?" She understands the machine is huge.

"With the slaver's ship," he replies, his eyes shifting to what lies ahead.

Sylvia blinks and refocuses on Pogues. He hops forward a short way as he sniffs side to side. "How do you know where the machine is?" she asks forcing herself not to look into his eyes.

"A Draoi ársa landed on Terra Verte," he tells her in a deep solemn voice. She has to bite her lower lip to not look up into his eyes as he speaks. "Her ship tore apart as it entered the atmosphere but the stasis capsule she slept in remained intact. From her I learned of the original machine."

Sylvia waits for him to say more when she hears a single hoot from Pogues. She halts and moves behind a tree. She waves at Rex to get behind a tree when she sees him digging through the pine needles that carpet the ground. He picks out some stones and puts them into his left hand which he clenches shut. His eyes scan the surrounding area.

"Hoot hoot," comes quietly through the air from Pogues. Her heart thudding rapidly she steps beside Rex.

"The four other Children of Myth machines can be destroyed," he tells her as he gazes ahead. "The original cannot."

"But the Draoi ársa only told you that the machine was here, on Lilly," she whispers. "How did the slavers find out?"

"Thrain," she hears his rumbling voice say with savagery. "I thought he was a Child of Myth because of his size and muscularity. And his eyes. Implants, fake eyes, won't work for long on Terra Verte. But his aren't fake; they were grown from a Child of Myth clone and abstracted to replace his."

"What do his eyes look like?" Sylvia asks. She starts to shiver. Would they be Miya's eyes?

"Not like yours," Rex replies. She waits as he glances around while tossing one of the stones with his right hand. "The eyes of a falcon."

"I have heard of the falcon, they live farther north. I don't want to meet this Thrain," She says looking up into his eyes and wishing she hadn't.

"There is a good chance you will, when we leave this place." There is a determination in his voice that makes her want to stay near him. He moves closer to Pogues and she follows.

Raven catches up to them. Around Rex she has completely forgotten about Raven. He holds the staff with the sack attached with drips of sweat falling off the tips of his bangs. She smells the acidic smell of heavy sweat from his body. An excitement fills her as he stands near. Her mind wants to forget the task ahead of them and wishes they were near a river or a lake with a sandy beach so they can swim before exploring one another more intimately on the shore.

"Hoot!" she hears Pogues call just ahead through tall redwood cedars.

Her ears twitch. Large things are nearby. She steps behind a tree with Raven. Rex slips behind his own tree.

"Let me have a weapon," Raven pleads to her in a whisper.

"Take the sack off the staff," she whispers back as she listens to the closing footfalls of very large creatures.

Without her permission Raven puts down the staff with the sack still attached and slips from behind the tree. She can hear his soft footsteps move closer to the coming creatures. He returns a few moments later gasping and his eyes bulging. "These are not the goblins I saw in the drawings from ancient texts," she hears him say to himself. "These are giants with heavy eyebrows, and an oversized orang-utan belly and long arms." He stares at Sylvia. "They have the faces of a bat but their heads are rounded like a human's."

"Shhh," Sylvia admonishes him.

"Their oversized head, feet and hands suggest acromegaly Sylvia," he continues. "That suggests they are going to be extremely strong!"

She puts her right hand over his mouth. She realizes her hearing is far superior to his. "They are almost here," she whispers into his ear.

In a flash he unties the sack from the short staff. At that moment Sylvia realizes she doesn't have a weapon!

The heavy footsteps grow louder and clearer. Sylvia doesn't know if the Vale de Coníferas goblins know where they are or if they are coming for them but she doesn't think so. The footsteps stop and she hears voices so deep their words are hard to grasp.

"The orc traders say the captured humans told them other humans landed on the other side of Mons Montis," one voice rumbles.

"In the little people's territory or the hated dwarves and elves?" another asks.

"We'll find out."

Sylvia hears other chattering but nothing she can make out until one of the Vale de Coníferas goblins speaks nearby. "What did the orcs do with the humans?"

"Muds," the original speaker says with a chuckle, "says their heads are on stakes, and their bodies are steaks." She starts to shake uncontrollably. *Please don't do anything*, she thinks as she glances at Raven who is grasping the short staff tightly in his right hand.

Lilly protects the Children of the Forest, she sings in her head as her heart pounds. The heavy steps get closer. *Gold River sings to us all day long*, her right hand grabs onto the bark of the redwood. *Close your eyes leanaí, you're safe,* a shadow longer and wider than Rex's presents itself to her. She sees Raven's back tense.

He screams savagely and jumps into the air as he swings the staff. Sylvia stares in terror as she hears the Vale de Coníferas goblin roar with rage. Raven's body is knocked backwards and she hears it thump against the ground. An orang-utan arm with an oversized human hand appears before her. The lumpy head of the goblin turns to reveal bat eyes that blink down at her while its knobby mouth snarls savagely in her direction. Its legs are thick with black bear fur and oversized human feet. She steps back as the massive hand shoots out at her.

The hand falls away before reaching her. The cruel bat eyes blink with confusion. Sylvia rapidly steps back as the tumorous head lolls to one side and the giant body falls first to its knees then face first onto the ground. She sees Rex helping Raven to his feet. Darkness is arriving fast and that frightens her even more. Her eyes sometimes light up if she stares into pure darkness too long. She rushes over to help Raven.

"I don't hear any more of them," she whispers to Rex. "I can smell their acidic odour but—." As she speaks she sees the goblins' huge forms lying in juxtaposed positions all around.

"We need more stones," Rex whispers back.

Sylvia remembers Pogues and Laurent. She sniffs the air and her ears twitch. She follows the deer scent of Laurent to a nearby giant red cedar. As she gets nearer she can also make out the musty smell of Pogues.

"We didn't know what to do," Pogues tells her as Laurent stares dumbfounded at the fallen goblins.

"They're only stunned," Rex warns.

"Right of the moon, when we can see it," Pogues says in a hushed voice.

"Can you continue Raven?" she asks.

"Yes," he replies sounding dazed, "but I would be more useful with a real weapon."

"Carry the sack," she commands with a calmness she doesn't feel. "We don't want to leave any traces."

Raven looks at the fallen goblins then back at her.

"We need the food," she tells him with a nod towards the sack. "Single file for now," she tells the others.

Pogues takes lead while Rex gathers more stones. Sylvia feels the ground with her feet as she walks and grabs whatever stones have pushed up through the dense carpet of pine needles.

She can still smell the thick odour of sweat from the Vale de Coníferas goblin's bodies mixed with the burning flesh of deer and other creatures she cannot name. Every so often she sees fires and long shadows. Over the fires are dark images of a spit and something cooking on it. She wonders how long will the Vale de Coníferas goblins Rex stunned stay unconscious? She glances back and sees Raven struggling with the sack. She goes back and takes the staff with the sack. She can just make out the look of defiance on his face but he relents. They can't afford to argue or even whisper while they hurry through the Vale de Coníferas goblin's territory.

Four more days of travelling and the redwoods grow less dense as the sun rises and she notices a stream not more than twenty paces across. Rex steps into the water. She glances around, terrified a Vale de Coníferas goblin will see him. He takes one step and stops before continuing. He moves diagonally before his shoulders sink under the water.

"Can you swim?" Raven whispers into her ear.

"Not well, water gets into my ears," she admits feeling exhausted and terrified.

"I will go first," he offers. "You follow only if my chest stays above the water." His voice sounds strained and there is pain in his eyes.

Sylvia nods. Pogues plops into the water and she sees his head stay just above the surface. Across the stream Rex stands with water dripping from his clothes as he tosses a stone in his right hand. She hears rustling in the woods behind her but not enough to know if it is heading in their direction. Raven steps into the water and she follows holding the staff and sack. Laurent comes up behind her and she feels safer.

Her ears twitch and the rustling sound grows louder. She can distinguish four separate footfalls and smell the stench of thick body odour. "Hurry," she tells Raven. He winces as he finds his footing. She hears branches being pushed apart. Rex throws a stone. Raven starts to turn.

"Go!" Sylvia admonishes him. Raven falters. Laurent moves ahead and grabs the back of Raven's collar dragging him to shore while Sylvia struggles with the staff and sack.

Something hits the sack pushing her forward into the water. She glances back and sees four Vale de Coníferas goblins snarling in her direction. None step into the water but each carries three javelins. The staff and sack float away with one of the javelins sticking out of it. She sees a fifth goblin sprawled on the ground and starts dog paddling towards the shore. Near the bank she stands up and hurries through the water. She sees Rex throw another stone; he looks frustrated and she can only imagine he missed.

Laurent drags Raven onto the bank and steps back into the water towards her. Rex throws another stone and she hears a deep rumbling roar of pain from across the stream. A javelin just misses her right cheek. She starts to climb to shore when another javelin flies past her and tears into Raven's left leg.

As Laurent pulls her from the water, Rex runs to Raven and hefts him over his shoulders.

They hurry past weeping willows and sumac. Sylvia leads them around a patch of thistly burdock. She halts by an outcropping of large, moss covered boulders.

Rex puts Raven down. "What do you use for wounds?" he asks.

Sylvia looks desperately around. "My sack had comfrey and moss in it but it's gone." She grabs a handful of moss off a rock. She sees little bugs in it and lets it fall to the ground. "Laurent?" she asks.

He searches through his sack. "Here is some comfrey and moss Abnoba." He hands her a small satchel.

"When I pull the javelin out," Rex instructs her, "you must quickly stuff in the moss on both sides of his leg then cover it in comfrey and tie it."

Sylvia nods as she searches for a string.

Rex tears off the sleeves of Raven's green shirt. He ties them together and passes them to Pogues. "Fast," he says in his deep mesmerizing voice. He places a stick in Raven's mouth. Sylvia sees the two men's eyes meet in understanding.

Rex yanks out the javelin, point first. Sylvia shoves moss into the hole on either side of Raven's bleeding leg as best she can as he twitches in pain. She covers the moss with wide comfrey leaves and Pogues uses the sleeves to tie the leaves in place.

"What now?" Sylvia asks as she caresses Raven's forehead.

"I don't think the goblins will come here," Rex says. He leads Sylvia around the boulders to where a large cherry tree grows amongst birch and poplar trees.

Oh, no! she thinks. Shoved onto sticks as tall as Rex are five human heads. "Orc land," she whispers.

"How long until we reach the sanguinarians' territory?" he asks.

"Another four days," she hears Pogues say from behind her.

"He can't go with us," Rex says glancing at Raven.

"I'll stay," Pogues says. "I'll gather supplies for your return and change his dressings."

"Keep him in the sun to dry out the wound, if you didn't know that already," Rex tells him.

"And out of the rain," Pogues finishes for him. "I'll make a shelter against the boulders and camouflage it."

"Better he doesn't see the heads," Rex adds.

Sylvia doesn't like this idea. Pogues is the most knowledgeable of them. "No," she says.

"Yes, I am the slowest Abnoba." She stares into his green eyes with their elliptical pupils as he hops up to her. "And the best healer," he continues. "Rumbleton says the goblins and orcs gathered forces and fought against the dwarves and elves a thousand seasons ago. The orcs are more your height but they are also more human than the goblins and shrewder."

Sylvia gulps and nods her head. "Give the javelin to Laurent and I will carry his staff and sack," she says.

She hurries to Raven's unconscious form touching his chest first then kissing his forehead and smoothing back his hair. "Heal so you can take care of Pogues," she tells him.

She sees Rex squinting into the distance. The colours of his eyes mesmerize her. Now they look hazel with a rim of cobalt. But the meaning behind his stare is definite; they need to get going.

Chapter Four

Sylvia places the staff with Laurent's sack over her left shoulder and the three of them head into the orc's territory.

Oak trees replace the giant redwoods as the dominant trees. She looks up at the long leaves each with three branching divisions that end in three points. Acorns are just forming. Between the oaks grow smaller bitternut hickory with their small thin leaves, and black ash with their small rounded leaves. It's quiet and peaceful. She waits for a hoot from Pogues before remembering he isn't with them. A cool breeze blows through the early morning. Dew glistens off birdfoot trefoil. She sees a mauve bergamot and its tiny white flowers that are just beginning to bloom and the rounded yellow petals of barren strawberry.

The musky smell of spring soil makes her long for late summer when the scent of the flowers will fill the air. She just wants to lie down and rest. Trying to catch her breath she calls a halt. She is about to lean against the trunk of a chestnut tree to rest when she hears unfamiliar sounding footfalls walking leisurely towards them. "Hide!" she whispers.

She sees Laurent move behind a chestnut tree. He holds the Vale de Coníferas goblin's javelin that Rex removed from Raven's leg. Rex stands behind a sugar maple tossing a stone with his right hand. She needs a weapon. Why didn't she learn to use a weapon! She knows her legs are powerful but on the rare occasions when she uses them it is out of anger.

"We need an army," she hears a male voice say with a petulant snarl.

"Only half of us can have children—as the creator made us, and not all of our women's pregnancies come to term," a deeper male voice says.

Sylvia's ears twitch and she can make out eight separate footfalls. *Be brave my children, be stolid in your stance, the storm winds will pass.*" The song is one her mother used to sing to her and Miya when they were little during the occasional torrential storm that would howl through the forest.

A man wearing a pale yellow jerkin and olive green pants steps in front of her. His scent is new, like wet leather mixed with moist earth. She can see a side view of his face and round tympanum ears. The side profile of the nose reminds her of a frog's jutting, upright nose. She looks down at his hand that clasps onto a cudgel made of bone. It is slick and mottled with green skin and black circles. How could Pogues be half human half toad while this orc appears to be a mottled combination of both human and frog?

Laurent knows how to move with stealth, hiding in shadows but she isn't sure if Rex does. She doesn't hear any commotion as the orcs continue to walk past. When the orcs' footfalls fade she peeks around the trunk. "Laurent, Rex?" she whispers.

Laurent steps away from his tree. He is soaked in sweat and shaking. Rex appears near her from another tree. "I don't know how to fight," she admits.

"That's why Pogues and I came along," Laurent tells her in his deep, solemn voice.

"I'll teach you in the sky," Rex assures her.

"Let's move on," she says. There is no time to ponder the very tall man's words.

"Rivers flow south from the forest," Laurent tells her. "The danger will be picking up Pogues and the human." She hears the distrust in his voice.

"That would be the quickest way to go home," she agrees glancing and listening and smelling in every direction. The movement through the dense area of the forest is slow. The river would be much faster.

"What happens when we find the Creator's original machine?" Laurent asks as they stay to the denser parts of the woods.

Bumblebees buzz by her nose and grasshoppers are just starting to hop around. She glances at Rex as she pushes branches from a hemlock bush away from her face.

"The ship I came in had a device and the one you call Daft kept it inside the pod." Rex answers, keeping his rumbling voice quiet.

"And?" she asks moving more branches away.

"I will connect it to Smide's machine and we will transport it." She watches in frustration as he moves faster without saying more.

Sylvia glances at Laurent and sees him shrug. She takes a swig of her water. How is Raven she wonders? Everyday her nerves grow worse; she just wants to soak in the eddies of Gold. But most of all she wants her sister back!

At twilight she calls a halt for the day. They are in a small opening in the thickest part of the forest made by boulders and a natural spring that flows east down a hill to a stream.

She awakes to the faint sound of movement. Listening more intently she realizes it is Rex. He is near one of the boulders, the growing dawn light giving his flawless skin a cobalt blue sheen. His feet and hands move together in synchronized motions. Every press and pull of his arms and every lean of his legs are slow; a mesmerizing dance of perfect fluidity. He steps with one foot as the other's heel rises. She hardly notices when the movements speed up to a blur. For a moment he seems invisible and she realizes just how fast he is able to move.

The sheen on his body should have aroused her desires but it doesn't. She stares at his statuesque stance with his chin tilted up, looking into the sky—for something. His eyes fall on her and she shudders. He splashes water from the spring onto his body and she watches.

"Why am I mesmerized but not wantonly attracted to you?" she asks in a whisper. He hesitates in his washing and she knows he has heard her.

"I think you should wake your friend up Abnoba," his voice rumbles over to her.

It dawns on her that what she feels around him is awe; like a small child feels towards their father, because to them their father is perfect and they want him to praise them. She rolls over to look at Laurent who is sleeping only a few feet away. "Laurent," she calls.

His brown eyes stares groggily back at her. "I heard."

Sylvia is relieved they haven't encountered any orcs but she is weary about the constant traveling.

"We should save the food we have left and catch fresh fish," Laurent suggests to her as the forest thins and more boulders appear. Sylvia hears a river flowing nearby and sees the top of a large hill not far off.

"I think we are nearing the sanguinarians' territory," she says. "Use the javelin to catch some fish. You can cook them while Rex and I keep watch."

"I'll make a javelin," Laurent replies and she hears hesitancy in his voice.

She turns to him. "Why?"

Laurent shows her the tip of the javelin Rex removed from Raven's leg. She inspects it closer and notices that it glistens dark red. "I think its poison," he says.

She thinks of Raven's leg. "No!"

"It might not be," she hears Laurent say but his voice betrays his belief that it is.

They have left Pogues and Raven behind, and the one called Daft is likely stirring up trouble back at the forest. "Why don't we forget the machine," she says shivering with dread.

"If it's no longer here Delve Mining has no reason to waste so many resources coming to Lilly," Rex's voice rumbles behind her. "And if they do capture it, more of your people will be made into slaves to work the mines of different worlds, and to die fighting other Children of Myth, along with humans, animals, and robots, as gladiators."

"I'm just so tired and worried," Sylvia admits.

"I need to keep going," Rex tells her and walks on.

"I don't want to lose my children to the slavers," Laurent tells her and he follows the King.

Chapter Five

By nightfall Sylvia can hear numerous voices. The snarling sounds of orcs and a new accent. Replying to the orcs is a soft, sweet sounding voice that drips of positivity and sensuality. "We would like to see the spaceship you found," she hears an effeminate voice telling the orcs.

"I would love to show it to you," replies a male orc voice that sounds like it is struggling to sound sarcastic. "But we need you to join us to defeat the dwarves and elves first."

"They are not so very dangerous," the effeminate voice continues. "Forget them and show me the ship. I can offer you better things than war."

"Yes," the orc replies lethargically.

She feels a soft touch to her right shoulder and jumps. Laurent points towards the voices then his chest. Sylvia nods. Not far away she sees Rex hunched down with his right hand clasped around a stone. She goes over to him and whispers, "Can you hear them?"

"Barely," he admits.

"They want the slaver's ship that landed here," she tells him.

"There were only five heads on stakes and yet there were two groups of six slavers when we left the

mother ship," he says thoughtfully. His engulfing eyes
stare down at her, "These sanguinarians must have
kept the sixth slaver alive."

"What happens if they get to the ship?"

"Incubus and succubus are known to deceive and
enchant in mythology," he tells her quietly. "If they
kept the slaver alive and he knows how to fly the ship."
He stops speaking.

"Yes?"

"I don't know," he replies. "Will the sanguinarians
join the slavers? Conquer them? Or will the slavers kill
them?"

Sylvia glances into the darkness and sighs. She
can hear the sanguinarian with the effeminate voice
manipulating the orcs. *What would happen if some of
them join with the slaver on his ship* she wonders? "Do
we need the second ship?"

"No, but we do need the mother ship to transport
the Children of Myth machine to Terra Verte," he
replies.

"What about these Dreadnought Satellites?" She
doesn't understand technology but she needs to.

"The Draoi ársa gave me the code to halt the
Dreadnoughts' guardian technology but it has a safety

reboot. We only have a short time to move the machine before the program starts up again."

"What happened to her?" Sylvia asks as she listens for Laurent's footfalls.

"Thrain captured her as well as me." Rex's baritone voice carries deep anger. Sylvia watches as he turns his gaze from her to the sky.

"Where is she?" Sylvia asks.

"I heard some of the slavers say they were taking her to Sårad Värld, a world with one of the Children of Myth machines."

"Can more machines be built?" She asks. A sense of hopelessness fills her.

"Perhaps," he answers, "But unlikely. It's extremely dangerous."

"What will she do?"

"Try to escape and destroy it," he answers matter-of-factly.

Sylvia knows by Rex's tone of voice that the conversation is over. She hears Laurent's soft footsteps grow louder. The moonlight outlines his stern eyes. "The sanguinarian is...enthralling in both his voice and looks," he says with a shake of his head.

"What does he look like?" Sylvia asks.

"The creator had an affinity towards bats I think," he tells her with a hushed voice. "He wears strange clothing and there is a wide hump on his back but it doesn't force him to lean forward. His ears are fleshy and pointed. When he smiles it is charming but for the two overly long canine teeth." *Like a bat's*, Sylvia thinks. "His eyes are pale blue," Laurent continues, "And his skin and hair are so translucent he shimmers pink in the moonlight."

"We should avoid these sanguinarians," Rex's baritone voice whispers with a thoughtful tone.

"Are my eyes shining green?" Sylvia asks.

"No," Laurent replies, "I only see that when you are sending a message through the trees or excited."

"Let's go then," she says staying hunched and moving through the brush with the help of the moonlight.

"I hear something," she says holding up her left arm. The sanguinarian is saying something to the orcs.

"An animal?" one of the orcs asks languidly.

"Not sure, my friend," she hears the sanguinarian reply. There is a pause before he continues with, "But we should investigate."

"They're coming," Sylvia says trying desperately to keep her voice down.

"Go ahead," Rex whispers.

She walks on as quickly and quietly as she can. Laurent stays slightly behind her.

"What is this beautiful dark being I see?" the sanguinarian asks. Sylvia stops, her heart pounding, as she listens then hears three thuds. She glances back and sees in the moonlight Rex carrying under his left arm the unconscious form of a man with shimmering pink skin. His bones are visible through the skin of his hands.

"Do you have rope?" Rex asks Laurent. Sylvia puts down Laurent's staff and sack and watches as Laurent searches inside it. He pulls out a length of sisal string. Rex takes it from him and deftly ties the sanguinarian's wrists and ankles. He pulls a square shaped cloth from a pocket in the sanguinarian's clothing and covers his mouth with it then ties it behind his head. Rex puts a leaf from a catalpa tree over each of the sanguinarian's eyes and uses what is left of the string to tie it. Sylvia wonders how he knows how to do this. "He can still hear so be careful what you say around him," Rex warns as he tosses the limp figure over his shoulders.

"What is his clothing?" Sylvia asks.

"Over his shirt is a vest," Rex tells her, "And over that a cape."

"What is the cape for?"

She sees Rex feel under the cape. "He has wings."

Sylvia leans closer to the unconscious face as the moonlight brings out his pallid features. The pointed canines have pierced the cloth. At the tips of the canines she notices dark spots that look like holes.

"Legend says the sanguinarians can infect others with one of two viruses when they bite them," Rex tells her with an amused sound to his voice, "and change them into obedient servants or another sanguinarian."

Sylvia moves away. "You think that is true?"

"I don't think Smide had the technological information to do that but life always implements itself into science, so be careful." Staring into the moonlight he starts to move on. "The orcs will awaken soon, or more might show up."

As dawn arrives Sylvia hears groaning. She sees Rex put down the sanguinarian.

Rex, keeping an eye on his captive goes over to her. "Can you hear any orcs or his like?" he asks pointing at the sanguinarian.

Sylvia's ears twitch. Wind rustles the forming leaves and rattles the branches. She hears a deer. "No," she whispers.

Rex unties the cloth over the sanguinarian's mouth. "Is that you most perfect human?" the effeminate voice asks in gasps.

"Where is the human you keep alive?" Rex asks in such an enchanting voice Sylvia just wants to sit near him and listen.

"He escaped the orcs and we found him cold and shivering at the bank of the river," the sanguinarian replies with an entrancing voice. "Zorlan has him chained in the tower with the other feed animals."

"What does Zorlan wish to do with him?" Rex asks in a smooth, hypnotic baritone.

"We are getting overpopulated," the sanguinarian replies with his mouth partially open so that Sylvia can see all the sharp teeth within. "We will go into space as the Creator's favourites."

"You are the favourites?" Rex asks.

"Yes, the Creator made us just before he died. Zoltan told us that we are the most human of his creations." The sanguinarian's head lolls to the left. "I will join him," he continues before drifting to sleep. Rex gags him again.

"We need to save this human?" Sylvia asks. She sees a consternated look on Laurent's serious face.

"No," Rex replies. "We need to get one of those orcs and see if they can be swayed to tell us where the pod is." She and Laurent follow him as he heads back towards the orcs they heard earlier.

"Tell me again what happens if they leave Lilly?" Sylvia whispers to him as she tries to keep pace.

"The sanguinarians and Delve Mining will become terrifying allies or horrific enemies."

"Will slavery end after all the machines are destroyed?" she asks, her heart pounding with hope.

"No," he replies. "Slavery is a state of mind. If an individual or individuals can teach toddlers to be servants the toddlers often know no better. That's where the machines are convenient for the slavers. Children of Myth are created without parents so they only know what the slavers tell them."

"Slavery is horrible," Sylvia says thinking of her sister, Miya.

"Worse is to be used for experiments," Rex says and she hears a hiss in his voice.

"Experiments?"

"Children of Myth who are created are often used for experiments to determine whether a food or drink is healthy for human consumption, or if a type of clothing will cause a skin rash."

"Can it be stopped?" she asks feeling helpless as a knot grows in the pit of her stomach.

"If the machines are destroyed or incapacitated there will be less slavery in this galaxy."

"I want my sister back!" Sylvia cries out as tears stream down her cheeks.

"We will look for her," Rex assures her.

The two orcs Rex had knocked unconscious before capturing the sanguinarian are sitting on a fallen log rubbing their foreheads where a noticeable swelling protrudes.

Rex bends down and asks into her ear, "Are there others?"

Sylvia listens intently. She can hear other orcs but they are a distance off. She glances at Laurent. He shrugs his shoulders. "No," she whispers to Rex.

"Stay here," he tells her and she watches as he crouches down and makes his way behind the two orcs.

She hears a thud and one of the orcs falls face forward onto the ground. The other starts to turn but Rex is upon him with his hand covering the orc's mouth and nose. She sees the orc twitching before falling unconscious beside his comrade.

Sylvia's ears twitch and she hears other orcs coming closer. Rex turns in her direction and nods. He picks up the orc he has suffocated into unconsciousness and throws him across his shoulders. With the Vale de Coníferas goblin's javelin in his hands she sees Laurent stand near the other orc. Sylvia shakes her head at him. They will not kill just for the sake of killing. Laurent bows his head and lowers the javelin. She shifts the staff across her shoulder so the weight of the sack feels more comfortable and follows after the King.

Rex hesitates by a stream surrounded by weeping willows, sumac, and dogwood. He splashes water onto the orc's face with one hand while he grasps the orc's neck in his other.

"You are a child of the night?" the orc asks in gasps.

"Where is the human pod?" Rex asks ignoring the orc's question.

The orc's dark eyes dart from side to side.

"You will live if you show me," Rex assures the orc with his mesmerizing baritone voice.

"And what of my people?" the orc asks. "The Incubus will use us as feed if you take it."

"I won't take it," Rex replies letting go of the orc's neck.

The orc massages his neck. He glances at Sylvia and Laurent. Sylvia feels shivers up her spine as the orc's eyes turn to her and linger on her body. Without a word the orc walks away from the stream. She sees Rex walking directly behind him with a stone clenched in his right hand.

Her mouth is dry and her legs are cramping. Sylvia just wants to rest as the sun reaches its zenith. Standing higher than the tree tops she sees the pointed top of a large metallic object. The orc walks faster. She can hear the sound of other orcs nearby. She hurries forward.

Rex glances her way before dashing ahead. He grabs the orc by the neck and the orc crumbles to the ground unconscious. "The pod is open but there are a number of orcs near it," he tells her.

She guesses he can see a lot more than she can with his greater height. He squints and his head turns in a semi-circle. She watches as he counts how many stones remain in his left pocket. There is a blur of movement and Sylvia hears multiple thuds. Seven orcs now lie on the scorched ground around the pod. Rex dashes inside it and she and Laurent follow.

Six metal chairs with vinyl padding face towards a central table with a round console. Rex is taking out a device from one of his pockets. He slides it into a slot in the console. Blue lines appear in a seemingly random pattern until Sylvia is able to make out three dimensional images. Rex's right hand's fingers are a blur as they touch the lights. Sylvia glances at Laurent. He stands frozen in place with his mouth open and eyes wide in awe. Rex touches one spot three consecutive times. "Let's go," he says.

"Where?" Sylvia asks, hoping they can return to Pogues and Raven.

"We need to find the machine," he replies ducking out of the pod's entrance and hurrying down its ramp.

"I'm trying Abnoba," Laurent says behind her, his deep voice sounds exhausted, "But my body can't keep going."

"Let's get into the forest first," she says, feeling her own exhaustion.

She sees Rex picking up his stones. "We need to rest soon," she tells him.

He nods and they head into the denser part of the forest. Sylvia sees that Rex is heading back towards where they left the sanguinarian. A short time later she calls a halt and collapses onto the ground with the staff and sack.

Rex scans their surroundings. "I'll return soon," he says.

"I hope he stays gone for a while," Laurent says as he plops down beside her.

"I'm worried about Pogues and Raven," Sylvia tells him as she digs into Laurent's sack for food.

"Yes, and my family and what that one called Daft is doing."

She smiles at him and hugs his wide shoulders. "We'll finish this and return by the river, I promise."

Twilight is coming when Rex returns carrying the same sanguinarian over his shoulders. "He should awaken soon," Rex tells her as he lays the sanguinarian onto the soft ground between two hazelnut trees. Laurent offers him some of the dried fish still remaining and Sylvia watches in astonishment how fast Rex devours it.

When the sun sets and the moon peers down Sylvia notices the sanguinarian stirring. He is trying to say something through his gag. Rex removes the gag.

"I need sustenance," the sanguinarian pleads.

"Do you know where the Children of Myth machine is?" Rex asks.

"Yes, but I need food." The effeminate voice's begging tone makes Sylvia ache for the man.

"Soon," Rex promises, "but we need to go to the machine to get it."

"It's closed," the sanguinarian says in a faraway voice. "The Creator asked our ancestors to carry him into it. When they set him down on a cot just inside the machine he pulled out some device from his shirt pocket and told our ancestors to wait outside. They saw him push something on the device and the machine rose slightly up into the air. They tried to enter but something invisible blocked them."

Sylvia sees Rex's eyes grow thoughtful in the light of the moon and stars. "Is it still hovering in the air?" he asks.

"Yes, and I will show you but I need sustenance." The sanguinarian's pleading tone makes Sylvia feel terrible inside.

Rex cuts the sanguinarian's ankles loose but not his hands. He leaves the leaf blindfold on. "Go," he says.

The sanguinarian gets to his feet. He stumbles a few paces until he walks into a tree. "We need time," Rex calls to him, "or I would cut loose your hands." Rex eats more of the fish and dates. "We have to hurry!" he tells Sylvia when he is finished.

"To the machine?"

"To your friend Pogues and the one you call Raven," he replies.

"And the forest," Laurent adds.

Rex leads them towards the stream as the sanguinarian makes a terrifying wailing sound. Sylvia hears strange female sounding howls reply. Her entire body shivers from the cries; she covers the opening of her ears with her hands.

Rex slows down and once she catches up tells her, "Keep moving Abnoba."

Sylvia shakes as if trying to remove something from her body. She wants to get away from the sanguinarian's wailing. She starts to jog. Laurent moves up beside her, his eyes wide and his head looking side-to-side. "Why aren't we getting the machine?" he asks.

"Because it's shielded," Rex replies from just up ahead. "It can't be moved now."

"For how long?" Sylvia asks, quickening her pace with her right hand held up in front of her to keep branches from slashing her face.

"Perhaps thousands of years," she hears him say as he veers left towards the stream.

"There's no way to get through this shield?" Sylvia feels perplexed; all this way for what? They couldn't take the machine away now.

"No," he replies glancing up into the sky. "We are both looking for someone but we have to save the Draoi ársa first." His gaze returns to the stream. "The direction it runs will lead to the river?" he asks.

"Yes," Laurent answers.

Sylvia feels drained, disheartened and full of rage. "I—want—my—sister—back!" she says straining to keep from shouting.

"Life doesn't often follow our wants," Rex replies.

"We'll need a raft or boat," Laurent says.

Sylvia's ears twitch. She hears numerous footfalls coming through the forest from both directions. "Keep moving!" she says shifting the staff with the sack onto her other shoulder.

"How much sisal string do you have left?" Rex asks as they use the starlight to follow the rippling current of the stream.

Sylvia glances at Laurent. "Almost none," he replies.

The stream opens into a river. Huts with straw roofs on poles cover the bank to either side. Fires, partially hidden deeper in the forest dot the night with an orange glow. There are hollowed out log canoes but nothing that will hold Rex.

As they move cautiously ahead Sylvia smells fish cooking and rabbit and it makes her heart ache.

Rex halts and puts his left arm out for them to stop. "There are enough canoes for everyone," he says.

Sylvia looks into Rex's dark, perfect face. A moment ago she felt hopeless, but the twinkle in his eyes, gives her a burst of strength.

She sees Laurent take out his knife. "I will cut the rope of the first canoe we come to, Abnoba, and you take it with the staff and sack. I will follow in the second canoe. If there is a paddle do not use it in the dark but let the current take you around any rocks." She follows him as he hunches down and heads towards the closest canoe.

Sylvia glances back at Rex and sees him heading in the opposite direction. "Where are you going?" she demands, terror filling her at losing the one person who can protect them best.

"I know where the river is Abnoba," Rex assures her, his eyes giving off a cobalt hue in the starlight. "I will meet you at the forest. There is something I need to do." She blinks and the night hides him from view.

Chapter Six

She whips her head around to find Laurent. He is hunched low holding onto the rope of one of the canoes. Keeping low she hurries to him. "Get in the canoe by holding the gunwales," he whispers to her. "Step into the centre then lay down on your back and I will push you off. Keep your body loose Abnoba or you might flip into the water."

Sylvia grabs a hold of the gunwales. The canoe's beam is wide but it still rocks making her feel helpless. Laurent holds the canoe until she is lying on the bottom. She can feel the sack against the tips of her ears and the staff against her left side. There is a slight jerk and the canoe starts moving. Her ears twitches and she hears Laurent's soft hoof steps move away. She sits up and can just see him cutting all the canoes loose. Her canoe passes the last one just as he is climbing into it. Grounding her teeth she lies down again. *It must have been one of the elves who taught him to canoe* she thinks. None of the dwarves would dare go into water over their heads.

Against her right hand she feels the handle of a paddle and recalls once seeing elven traders from a different forest hamlet travel through Gold in dugout canoes. They used the paddle with one hand atop the grip and one near the throat of the shaft. The canoe rolls to one side and she tenses. She forces herself to relax while her heart thuds painfully inside her chest. "*The full moon is a new moon*" she sings softly to calm her phobia of getting her ears soaked. "*Yellow says spring is here and the forest is awoken; red for the heat of summer when the flowers are full blossom; silver brings the change of colours and the leaves tumble to the ground; black and white when the deciduous sleep. The full moon is a new moon...,*" she sings the verses over and over as the current pulls her canoe forward.

Exhausted from the days of journeying and hiding she stares at the stars until her body goes numb. Her eyelids close and her mind drifts into dreams. She feels a jolt by her feet and grabs for the gunwales to steady the canoe as she sits up. Dawn is just arriving and she can see branches where the end of the canoe has struck the bank. The canoe pivots until she finds herself flowing backwards. She cannot let go of the gunwales as her hands refuse to loosen.

"Abnoba!" she hears Laurent call from behind her, "Stay low!"

Sylvia lowers herself back into a lying position in the canoe but she still refuses to let go of the gunwales. The canoe moves faster. For an instant she feels herself descending, in the next moment the stern of the canoe thuds into water and begins floating faster again.

"There's no one in those canoes!" she hears a snarling voice say from nearby.

"Let's gather them at the verengung where the water is much shallower," says another voice.

"Abnoba," she hears Laurent say before something softly bumps against her canoe. "Are you well?" he asks.

She sits up and looks all around. She and Laurent's canoes are floating in the middle of a wide section of river with the shore a bow shot away but too far for javelins. "The orcs are going to get us by the verengung," she tells him unable to keep the worry from her voice.

"I heard them but I couldn't make out their words," he says as the canoes continue to lightly tap against each other.

"They said the water is much shallower there." She glances from shore to shore for any movement.

"I will tie the bow of your ship to my stern but first you must turn around. Place the shaft of the paddle across the gunwales, that will help you balance." She observes Laurent as he takes out a paddle and shows her how to hold it. He grabs the bow of her canoe. Deftly he ties some of the sisal string to a hole carved just under the section of the gunwale closest to the bow and through the one on his stern. "Like the Delvin forest elves, the orcs must pull extra canoes with goods in them," he tells her.

"Who do they trade with, not the dwarves?" she asks.

"Maybe the sanguinarians or others farther north," she hears him reply with a shrug. "I'm going to tow you around. The greatest danger is when the current hits the port side."

"What should I do?" she asks wondering how deep the water is.

"Paddle on the port side--quickly," Laurent replies and with a solemn sigh starts paddling.

Sylvia holds up the paddle as Laurent has shown her. Grinding her teeth together she tries paddling. The string pulls taught and her movements become desperate and short. Be *calm* she tells herself. In the distance she sees the other canoes he has cut loose.

She paddles madly now as his canoe moves forward and hers turns.

"Can you hear me Abnoba?!" Laurent asks when her canoe is behind his.

"Yes!" she replies, trying to keep the canoe steady.

"Stroke with every second one I make but keep them synchronised. We want to get through the narrow passage before the orcs do to gather the canoes."

Sylvia keeps her eyes on Laurent's strokes. Once she has the cadence she glances at the shores. Every so often she sees orcs on the banks collecting pails of water or fishing and shouting towards them. As their speed increases she sees orcs push off in other canoes.

"The river is narrowing ahead," Laurent calls to her.

She wants to turn her head to see how close the orcs in the other canoes are but when she tries her canoe almost tips. Water lilies are everywhere, their white flowers brushing against the sides of her canoe. The river splits into numerous streams until it narrows and turns into the verengung. She looks into the water and can see the pebbly bottom. "Should we get closer to shore?" she asks. There is no reply and she asks again louder.

"No!" Laurent replies, "We may get stuck in the weeds. Only dip your paddle in slightly now, as I am."

Sylvia sees Laurent holding the shaft of his paddle farther out so that the blade only skims the water. *When will this be over* she wonders pinching her eyelids closed for a moment. She might be frightened but her determination is stronger. Her greatest concern is the orcs in the canoes. And Rex, why did he stay back?

The midnight sky turns from navy blue to slate blue as the red sun covers up the entire horizon, its reflection rippling in the current. In the centre of the verengung the other canoes swirl in broad circles because of an eddy. She sees the muscles on Laurent's back tense as he digs his paddle in with broad strokes. She follows his example.

Orcs trying to capture the circling canoes with hooks made of bone attached to long poles stop and stare at them. Sylvia feels all their eyes upon her. "What is that?" she hears a female orc ask pointing at her.

An orc in one of the canoes following them shouts, "Stop them!"

Laurent paddles madly now with long strokes. She copies him as some of the orcs plunge into the water with their long, hooked poles. Laurent pulls his paddle out of the water and uses the top of the handle to push one of the empty canoes away. The bow of Sylvia's canoe bumps into his stern and she places the shaft of her paddle across the gunwales to keep from tipping.

She sees Laurent steady his canoe before pushing another empty canoe out of the way. From behind she hears a bang followed by a splash. One of the orcs following them in a canoe must have capsized.

"Paddle!" she hears Laurent shout. She digs into the water as he does, moving the paddle side-to-side to stop the canoe from turning in the eddy. Ahead the river expands into rapids. "Let it pull you along," Laurent calls back to her taking his paddle out of the water.

They move faster and faster until the shoreline becomes a blur. The sun is glaring orange in the centre of the sky as they go around a bend. She recognizes the bank. This is where they left Pogues and Raven.

"Get ready Abnoba!" Laurent shouts back at her as he begins to paddle furiously. "Paddle on the starboard but only so you don't turn sideways!" He brings them closer and closer to the bank. She keeps her eyes on the other shore where the Vale de Coníferas goblins had thrown javelins at them.

They are almost to the shore when Laurent shouts, "Paddle port side!" She does, just as his canoe strikes the bank through a cluster of bulrushes. Her canoe bangs into his and almost turns sideways but Laurent leaps out of his canoe and grabs hers to keep it steady. "Get out and pull it farther ashore," he tells her as he lets go of hers and grabs onto the bow of his own canoe.

On the shore Laurent ties the canoes to a weeping willow root that has grown into the water as Sylvia falls to the ground gasping.

"Pogues!" she hears Laurent call in a muffled shout. He waits and calls again. Sylvia squeezes her eyelids closed. *Please don't let them be dead.*

"Here," she hears the familiar gulping voice of Pogues. She looks up and sees him standing just outside the bushes. She realizes this is the lean-to Pogues had said he would make.

"Where's Raven?" she asks.

"Here but not well Abnoba." She hears the worry in Pogue's voice.

"We have to go!" Laurent says. Sylvia turns to him and follows his gaze towards the distant canoes heading their way down the river.

"Can you paddle Pogues?" she asks considering his squat form.

"No Abnoba," he admits, "but I can balance very well."

"Pogues, you're with Laurent and we'll put Raven in my canoe," she says.

Pogues leads them into the lean-to where Raven lies pale and sweating with new leaves wrapped around his injured leg. Sylvia and Pogues lift him by the shoulder while Laurent takes his feet. Sylvia glances down the river and sees that the canoes are getting dangerously close. She bites her lower lip as they put Raven into her canoe with his feet on the bow seat and his head under the yoke. She sees Laurent looking intensely at her canoe. "What?" she asks.

"You and Pogues go together," he says with concern in his brown eyes. "I'm more familiar with canoeing than you Abnoba."

"Yes," she agrees. She puts her sack and staff into the canoe as Pogues climbs in. Laurent pushes them off. She wants badly to be with Raven but Laurent will have to be the hero on this trip.

Vale de Coníferas goblins appear on the portside shore as they paddle. None are carrying javelins but many pick up stones and throw them. Sylvia wants to paddle faster but forces herself to keep even strokes. Her shoulders are burning and her wrists ache. Pogues looks back at her with the eyes of someone who feels useless. She nods for him to keep his eyes forward.

The river begins to flow so fast she takes her paddle out of the water. "Are they safe?" she shouts through the roaring of the water.

Pogues glances back. "They are Abnoba," he tells her with a reassuring smile.

The land becomes rocky as they splash down small waterfalls that soak her from the spray. She glances to starboard and sees the tree covered form of Mon Montis. "Are the orcs following us?" she shouts.

Pogues peers behind once again and shakes his head. "I know where we are now," he tells her and she joyfully sucks in the confident sound of his voice. "We will have to portage to get to Gold, about an hour from now."

An hour passes and the rapids slow so Sylvia has to paddle again. The surrounding land does look familiar. They are in the forest now.

"Head towards those reeds!" Pogues shouts at her.

She paddles hard on the port side until she is deep into the reeds and the canoe refuses to budge. "Steady it for me," she says climbing out of the canoe. As she pulls the canoe closer to shore she hears the sound of reeds brushing against something. She can just see Laurent and his canoe. "Can you pull the canoe up yourself?" she asks Pogues, desperate to help Laurent get Raven out.

"I can," Pogues tells her rocking the canoe as he leaps into the water. She passes him the sisal string.

Raven is mumbling incoherently as she and Laurent drag his canoe ashore.

"We can get back faster," Laurent says, "If we tie together a stretcher." He digs into the sack and pulls out a folded canvas blanket and hands it to Pogues.

While Laurent and Pogues make a stretcher she feels Raven's forehead. It is sweaty and hot. "We'll have proper herbs soon," she tells him brushing his slick hair away from his forehead.

She sees Laurent with two sticks his own height. He puts the sticks under the blanket. She helps Pogues roll the sticks until they are tightly inside the sides of the blanket. Sylvia helps them place Raven onto it. "Laurent and I will carry him," she says, "and Pogues you keep the javelin and carry the sack."

Twilight is upon them as they reach the even darker depths of the woods. Sylvia's entire body aches. "Rest," she croaks out.

"I see you," says a playful and familiar lisping voice from high up in an oak tree.

"Daryl," she hears Laurent say with relief.

"Who is the pretty lapin with you?" Daryl asks and she feels her cheeks burn. "Abnoba, you are even more gorgeous all hot and sweaty," the sloth man shouts down.

Sylvia places her hands on the bark of the oak. She sees the green light from her pupils make two tiny branched images onto the bark as her pheromones course through her body and into the tree. The message will tell Lana someone is hurt and to bring healing salves. She kneels down to see how Raven is.

"We may have been followed by orcs on canoes." Laurent says.

"Ask Darryl to watch for Rex, too," she says as her palm feels the heat coming off Raven's forehead. She peers around and sees that it is too dark to continue.

Pogues hops up to her. "The fever is not a bad thing," he assures her, "Unless he becomes too hot. If that happens we can pour water from our skins onto him. There's a stream nearby if we need to place him in it."

She takes out a second blanket and places it beside Raven's stretcher. She reaches out with her right hand and places it over his. A feeling of doom ripples through her body as sleep overtakes her.

Was it a dream she wonders as she opens her eyes to a terrifyingly familiar sight. The sky is unnaturally dark. "Oh no," she whimpers. Raven is asleep but Laurent is fully awake and standing, staring into the sky. "Not now!" she says aloud.

Chapter Seven

Laurent stares at her with his solemn eyes. "They have returned," he says in a voice full of weariness. "I must get back to my family Abnoba."

She nods with wrenching devastation. Laurent turns away and walks briskly into the depth of the forest. Hopelessness fills her. There is no time to make a travois but the poles of Raven's stretcher are so heavy in her hands. *How long*, she wonders, *how long until they send more pods down to see what happened to the ones already here?*

Pogues hops up and grabs the other end. "I won't be as fast as Laurent but we'll get him as far as we can."

"Or leave him?" Sylvia asks looking up at the sky. "I don't think they will harm him and I don't know if we can save him." She sets down her end and Pogues does the same with his. Her right hand caresses Raven's sweaty forehead. She pours some water from her water skin into his mouth; more when she sees him drinking it. "We'll light a fire," she says. "So they'll have a beacon to him." She puts her hand on the trunk of an elm tree and sends warning pheromones throughout the forest.

Pogues brushes away any pine needles or old leaves from a circle of ground. He uses dried moss from the sack and flint stones to start the fire and makes a small tee-pee of sticks to keep it going. Sylvia kisses Raven's forehead.

"Yes, No, Maybe, Yes, No, Maybe" Sylvia sings as she and Pogues hurry towards the hamlet. *"Darlin' if you keep pulling off these petals of indecision"* she continues while glancing up at the darkening sky, *"you will kill this flower."* She bites down on her lower lip while tears pour down her cheeks. Raven's image disappears from her thoughts and she remembers her sister Miya kicking and screaming as the human slavers dragged her away. She will send someone when the humans have gone to see if Raven is still here. If Rex's words are true she will leave with him to find Miya.

Between the crowns of two birches she hears the sound of familiar flapping. Lana lands on a lower branch. "I have your herbs," Lana tells her in a sultry voice.

"They're coming," is all Sylvia manages to say. Lana's mouth opens and her eyes grow wide. "We left Raven for his people." Sylvia tells her before going quiet. In the darkness of the sky she sees a single dot of light head towards them.

"I will get them to him and make sure Daryl is on his way back to the hamlet," Lana tells her. "The one

Rumbleton called Daft has caused a great deal of trouble. He pleaded for water by desperately nodding at a water skin one of the young elves was holding. As soon as his gag was off he started saying how we are abominations and that we should kill ourselves because we are soulless monsters. The children are downtrodden and we are worried some of them will take their lives.”

“What did Rumbleton do to keep him quiet?” Sylvia asks in despair.

“He gagged him and Lent fed him psilocybin mushrooms but we fear the damage is done.” The lament in Lana’s voice fills Sylvia with grief.

“Let me know if Rex appears,” Sylvia says as she reaches up and touches her cousin’s left ankle. It gives her strength as Lana smiles down at her with sadness but also determination.

Sylvia hurries into the hamlet towards the secret place. She stops at a cluster of sumac and whistles an imitation of a robin’s song. Jezzel replies with the song of a nuthatch. Now that she knows the Children of the forest are safe she walks briskly towards the rocky caves near Gold where Rumbleton and Lent should be preparing for war.

Between a cluster of brambleberry bushes with their thorns and red fruit she sees what appears to be an impassable wall of granite. She moves along the brambleberry until she comes to a patch of sweet grass. On her hands and knees she crawls through the grass, reaching out with her left hand, until she feels the downward entrance.

Without light she crawls in. *Go left* she reminds herself when the tunnel splits into a Y. Her knees hurt from the roots and pebbles along the floor as she heads towards the sound of Rumbleton and Lent arguing in the musty hollow.

"We'll attack with our hammers first!" Rumbleton roars.

"We will shoot our arrows into them first and as they fall and are distracted you will attack," Lent replies with a calm but stern voice. "Shhh!" she hears Lent admonish.

"It's me," Sylvia tells them.

"Abnoba," Rumbleton says with relief in his voice.

"Lent is right," she says brushing the dirt off her legs and hands as she stands up. "Get near but let the elven archers fire on the humans first. We don't want to lose anyone."

"Aye," she hears Rumbleton say with a grumble.

Both Rumbleton and Lent's eyes give off a yellow glow. Her left hand feels around until it rests on one of Rumbleton's shoulders. Blindly she follows him out through a curtain of ivy into a sunlit opening surrounded by a hedge of hawthorn.

Rumbleton roars like the bears that live to the south and Lent whistles like a lark. Elves and dwarves pour out of their hiding spots amongst holly and boxwood. Sylvia sees either short or long hunting bows in the elves' hands. Five of the elves, including Lent carry the captured cross-bows from the human slavers. They will string them as soon as Daryl or Lana tells them the enemy is on its way. The dwarves in turn hold hammers with oak shafts and granite heads in their thick fingered hands.

"War!" Rumbleton yells and the dwarves raise their hammers over their heads and shout back in reply.

Sylvia's inner ear hairs tickle near a birch tree. She puts her palm on the bark of the tree and waits.

"Let the elves attack first," Sylvia reminds Rumbleton. "Be near enough to charge. They will have cross-bows this time." She remembers how the humans came with strange one-handed weapons the first time. After one or two shots of coloured lights that killed Children of the Forest instantly, yellow light came down from the skies burning the humans into dust that floated into the night air before drifting to the ground. She turns to Rumbleton, leaning close she whispers, "Where is Daft?"

"I bound him in the cave closest to the weeping willow where Gold bends to the west," Rumbleton replies with a voice full of hate. "He was corrupting one of the young elves. Told the kid he would kill his mother."

"And the elf boy?" Sylvia asks, her heart beating faster as she feels Lana's pheromones course through her palms. In her mind she sees a space pod much larger than the one Rex, Raven, and Daft arrived in land nearby. The image vanishes. "They're coming!" she shouts. She sees the elves head out with the dwarves close behind.

"His mother is watching him. He made it clear he wanted to kill Daft to protect his mother," Rumbleton tells her. "It's time Abnoba!" he says with a growl.

Sylvia hears the quiet rustling of leaves from a nearby bumble berry plant. It has to be an elf, dwarf, or one of Laurent's family members. She starts to step forward when a pointy eared woman rushes towards her.

"My boy is gone," Mentha shouts out her voice thick with worry.

Sylvia recalls what Rumbleton had said and tells Mentha, "Wait for him at your home." She hurries towards the cave where Rumbleton has Daft bound.

This is the absolute worst time for her to be searching for the boy but if he is intent on killing Daft she has to stop him or make sure he succeeds. She hears rustling nearby but cannot pick up any distinct scent. She follows the bend in Gold to a weeping willow at the base of a small hill with a cave. She yanks the curtain of lichen away from the cave's entrance.

The elbow to her forehead knocks her against the rocky ground of the bank. Dazed she stares up at Daft. He looks haggard from too little food and water but his blue eyes still shine bright with malice. Her first thoughts are for the boy. She rolls onto her feet and sways with dizziness. As Daft grabs at her she kicks at his groin.

His hand sweeps her foot aside. She can hardly breathe as his right hand clenches onto her throat. He glances up towards the sky as she chokes. He stares down at her with a cruel, gleeful smile. "They're here," he says in a raspy voice. "Told the freaky pointy ear that it was typical of your abominable species to kill

others who couldn't defend themselves, and he untied
me to fight me honourably." She feels his spittle against
her face. "Showed him who the better species is."

A midnight blue flash goes by her. She blinks and
sees Daft in the air with Rex's long fingers around his
throat. Daft says something and Rex puts him down.
With his fingers massaging his throat Daft says with a
hoarse voice, "Yield, I yield."

"Are you--," Rex says turning towards Sylvia.
Sylvia's eyes open with alarm as Daft kicks at the back
of Rex's left knee. In a flash Rex spins around and slaps
Daft across the face with the back of his hand. "You
dare attack me after you yield?!" Rex shouts.

Sylvia watches in terror as Rex grabs the top of
Daft's head with one hand while the other squeezes
Daft's throat. Rex twists Daft's head and she hears a
grotesque snap. Daft falls to his knees and stares in
shock as his neck swells.

Still shaking from the power and violence she has
just witnessed from Rex, Sylvia gets up and pulls the
lichen aside. Meltha's son stares up at her. He isn't
dead but his left arm and right leg are noticeably
broken. "Oh, you poor child," she says. "Be brave and I
will bring you help."

Rex appears behind her. Without a word he bends down and feels around the boy's arm. "Don't move," he says with a soothing baritone voice. To Sylvia he says, "He'll need a splint on both the arm and leg but there is no time now." He yanks the boy's arm from either side of the break and Sylvia wants to weep as the boy screams. "Keep still until we return," Rex warns as he yanks on the boy's leg and Sylvia sees the boy's eyes roll up and close. He is breathing but the pain must have knocked him unconscious. "Get the mother and I will find you soon," Rex tells her as he dashes out of the cave.

Sylvia strokes the boy's head but there isn't time to do more for him, she has a battle to fight. She hurries to the giant oak where Meltha lives. "Meltha," she calls softly up at the spherical wooden house Meltha and her late husband had grown. A ladder made of thick vines drops out of a hole at the bottom of the house and Sylvia waits as Meltha climbs down. "He is at the secret place by the giant willow where Gold bends," Sylvia tells her hurriedly. "He needs splints so bring binding and wood and food supplies. I want you to stay there until this battle is won."

"Yes Abnoba." Melta hurries back up the ladder and as she does Sylvia hurries towards the sound of the battle.

She can hear the twang of familiar and unfamiliar bows and cross-bows. Taking in a deep breath she runs in that direction. The artificial darkness in the sky makes her feel ill inside. *What if more pods come?* When the human slavers took Miya and other Children of the Forest there was no time to prepare. But this time they were ready. Sylvia sees the faint harlequin green outlines of two birch trees reflected on a beech tree ahead of her. Her rage hormones are surfacing even as her heart pounds in fear.

As she nears the battle she hears Rumbleton scream out "War!" Other dwarves shout out as they rush the humans. A whooshing sound fills the air and she can just make out Rex's very tall form through bushes as he throws stone after stone.

As the humans charge to meet the dwarves, Daryl and his family drop nets. The dwarves show no mercy. With their hammers they beat any human within the nets to death. She hears the twang of cross-bows from behind trees. Some of the dwarves fall to the ground, bolts jutting out of their writhing bodies. Other dwarves charge through the forest followed by elves with re-loaded cross-bows. She sees Rumbleton lead some of the dwarves farther into the woods. Lent and a group of elves spread out. Sylvia turns her attention to the wounded.

A young elf man grimaces with silent pain from the metallic cross bolt stuck through his left thigh. Mordid, one of the middle-aged dwarves lies on the ground, his chest still, with a bolt through his forehead. Sylvia feels helpless as she hunches down and peers through sumacs at the open surface where the space pod landed. Rumbleton, Lent and Rex are walking with other Children of the Forest towards the human bodies that lie strewn around it. She can do nothing for the battle so she returns to Mordid.

Her ears detect no breathing. She places her hand on his chest but it doesn't move. "I'm sorry," she says to his still form as tears burn down her cheeks. A dwarven woman, Betty, his wife, kneels down beside her and gasps. Sylvia watches in despair as Betty pulls the bolt from Mordid's forehead. Blood pools out and Betty tries to staunch the flow with her hands. Sylvia wraps her arms around her. "He's gone but he helped save us," she says soothingly.

"I know," Betty manages to say through sobs. "But it's so hard to bring children up alone."

"I didn't want anyone to die or be taken," Sylvia tells her feeling she failed.

"It's not you Abnoba," Betty tells her in an understanding voice. "Mordid would be proud that we stood up to them this time."

Sylvia runs her left hand through Betty's red hair. "You're not alone." Gulping in air she brushes away her tears and heads for the pod's opening.

Inside she finds Rumbleton, Lent and Rex. Rex's fingers are flowing over lines and dots of lights that hover in the air. This pod is much bigger than the other ones. She sees twelve chairs around a circular table. "Mordid is gone and many other dwarves are wounded," she whispers. She sees Rumbleton's lips purse and his head nod. "And at least one elf is badly wounded," she says with more clarity to Lent. "You two should go to your people."

The command is unmistakeable and she has one more before the day is over. Both Rumbleton and Lent leave the pod so she and Rex are alone. "We'll take this one," he tells her in a voice that sounds like quiet thunder.

"And the other two?" Sylvia asks.

"I found the sanguinarian and made a deal. They will take the one in the orc territory. The one that originally landed near your land should be covered and let be, for now.”

“Will the sanguinarians be enemies or friends?” she asks her eyes wandering around the strange interior of the pod.

“Or neutral,” Rex replies. “The mistake the slavers made was to think that Children of Myth are unintelligent or without feeling. Humans are notorious at looking upon other species that way.”

“All humans?” Sylvia asks chewing on her lower lip.

“Not all Abnoba but many.” Rex moves his fingers over some more of the lights. “That can change,” he continues. “Prejudice is most often taught from fear or misunderstanding. Humans are the one species that are reliant on other animals for clothing. So they claim they are better than the rest instead of admitting their dependency.”

“Is there food and water aboard?” she asks.

“Yes,” he replies touching more lights.

“And you have a plan?”

“You will need to use the slavers’ weapons once we are aboard the mother ship,” he tells her. His soul swallowing eyes turn to her. “I don’t think killing is avoidable.”

She thinks of her sister, the other Children of the Forest taken from their families, of the parents that died, and of Mordid who lost his life just now. "I can kill if it is just."

"Do what you need to do now Abnoba and I will meet you back here." His voice is gentle but dismissive.

Feeling as if her body is floating she walks out of the pod towards her people. The elves are collecting bolts from the humans' bodies and the ground where the battle took place. The dwarves are helping their wounded and building a makeshift stretcher for Mordid. Laurent and Pogues along with their families are already digging holes to bury the humans before disease sets in. She turns to an elven woman named Lila. "Have you seen Lana?" she asks.

"I saw her flying through the forest with a bag in her hand after the humans landed. She shouted down to me it was plantain and you would understand."

"Everyone!" Sylvia shouts. Slowly all the Children of the Forest halt what they are doing and look her way. "I am going to find my sister and the other Children of the Forest. I name Lana as Abnoba in my leave! Does anyone disagree?" She waits, searching the different faces. Some are full of glee that the humans are

defeated, others exhausted, and some mournful and
afraid.

"Lana!" Rumbleton shouts thrusting a fist in the
air. More and more of the Children of the Forest shout
out her cousin's name with their fists raised.

Sylvia presses her hand to an ancient chestnut
tree. "I cannot wait to tell her myself," she says to
Rumbleton and Lent. She hangs her silver necklace
with the onyx and quartz pebbles onto a low branch.

Rumbleton grabs her into a bear hug. "Will you
take my hammer?" he asks.

"No," she says crying. "There are other weapons
for me to use."

When she lets go of Rumbleton, Lent clasps her
hands in his. "Find her and the others," is all he says.

Sylvia glances all around at the diverse peoples of
the Children of the Forest. "I will remember," she tells
them hardly able to see them through her tears. "And I
will return." She freezes, not wanting to leave. But she
is an Abnoba, and fear does not rule her determination.
Grinding her teeth she turns and hurries into the pod.

Acknowledgements

Thanks to Leah Weir for reading and editing and Brad Harvey for doing a once over. To Samantha Borys for modelling and Randy Bugdale for the amazing artwork done in pencil crayon.

About the Cover Art

Samantha Borys
(model)
beabetteryou123@gmail.com

Loving mom & wife. Early Childhood educator & working towards Resource Consultant for the Early Years. Loves to hike, bike, swim, garden and many other activities with her family.

Owner of Be A Better You Essentials - DoTERRA Advocate. Using natural remedies in everyday life and healing the mind, body and soul through essential oils.

Randy Bugdale

(Artist)

I try to do stuff that I find interesting...most of the time.

Much of the stuff I've done has run a rather bizarre gamut of subjects like ads (and the occasional logo) for: various agricultural vet & feed suppliers, several bars, several bar bands, music stores, ballistic armour, cards for a wrestling game and many others. Add in portraits of people, portraits of their pets, portraits of their house, cars, and guitars.

There's also an odd smattering of stuff I've done just because I felt like doing it - or to see if I could-- like cartoons, ridiculously over-sized ink pictures of dragons, or carving things out of wood.

Mostly I do B & W pen and ink, some grey-scale pencil, the rare bit of vector art, and the very occasional use of colour.

Dan Watt

(author)

I mentioned to Sam what I was looking for on the cover of Sylvia and she took the picture herself while the wind was blowing in her hair. The picture was exactly what I was looking for. Randy wanted to continue working with pencil crayons. How he made Sylvia's eyes look exactly the way I wanted I don't know. However, he did find ink did not work with pencil crayon, so once again all the details are in Prismacolor pencil crayons.

Dan Watt can be reached at mythruin@gmail.com or his websites:

caedar-writing-artwork.com

mythruin.simplesite.com

Other books by Dan Watt (available through
Amazon Books as either e-book or paperback):

Queen of Caelum (the first book in the Children of
the Myth Machine series), fantasy/science fiction

Brackish (ship seven of the Future Wake series)
with Andy Watt, science fiction

Lucy & The Snivel Chair, mystery, science fiction

Hierarchy of the Undead: A Gothic Horror Musical,
based in Ireland and including many of Ireland's
famous and infamous mythological characters

Dragon: The Emerald of Light, a medieval spoof